HINDU GODS AND
HEROES

I0552619

HINDU GODS AND HEROES

STUDIES IN THE HISTORY OF
THE RELIGION OF INDIA

LIONEL D. BARNETT

Srishti
PUBLISHERS & DISTRIBUTORS

Srishti Publishers & Distributors
Registered Office: N-16, C.R. Park
New Delhi – 110 019
Corporate Office: 212A, Peacock Lane
Shahpur Jat, New Delhi – 110 049
editorial@srishtipublishers.com

First published by
Srishti Publishers & Distributors in 2018

Printed at Repro Knowledgecast Limited, Thane

Contents

Preface

The following pages are taken from the Forlong Bequest lectures which I delivered in March last at the School of Oriental Studies. Owing to exigencies of space, much of what I then said has been omitted here, especially with regard to the worship of Siva; but enough remains to make clear my general view, which is that the religion of the Aryans of India was essentially a worship of spirits—sometimes spirits of real persons, sometimes imaginary spirits—and that, although in early days it provisionally found room for personifications of natural forces, it could not digest them into Great Gods, and therefore they have either disappeared or, if surviving, remain as mere Struldbrugs. Thus I am a heretic in relation to both the Solar Theory and the Vegetation Theory, as everyone must be who takes the trouble to study Hindu nature without prejudice.

L. D. B.

May 29, 1922.

CHAPTER 1

THE VEDIC AGE

Let us imagine we are in a village of an Aryan tribe in the Eastern Panjab something more than thirty centuries ago. It is made up of a few large huts, round which cluster smaller ones, all of them rudely built, mostly of bamboo; in the other larger ones dwell the heads of families, while the smaller ones shelter their kinsfolk and followers, for this is a patriarchal world, and the housefather gives the law to his household. The people are mostly a comely folk, tall and clean-limbed, and rather fair of skin, with well-cut features and straight noses; but among them are not a few squat and ugly men and women, flat-nosed and nearly black in colour, who were once the free dwellers in this land, and now have become slaves or serfs to their Aryan conquerors. Around the village are fields where bullocks are dragging rough ploughs; and beyond these are woods and moors in which lurk wild men, and beyond these are the lands of other Aryan tribes. Life in the village is simple and rude, but not uneventful, for the village is part of a tribe, and tribes are constantly fighting with one another, as well as with the dark-skinned men who often try to drive back the Aryans, sometimes in small forays and sometimes in massed hordes. But the world in which the village is interested is a small one, and hardly extends beyond the bounds of the land where its tribe dwells. It knows something of the land of the Five Rivers, in one corner of which it lives, and something even of the lands to the north of it, and to the west as far as the mountains and deserts, where live men of its own kind and tongue; but beyond these limits it has no knowledge. Only a few bold spirits have travelled eastward across the high slope that divides the land of the Five Rivers from the strange and mysterious countries around the great rivers Ganga and Yamuna, the unknown land of deep forests and swarming dark-skinned men.

In the matter of religion these Aryans care a good deal about charms and spells, black and white magic, for preventing or curing all kinds of diseases or mishaps, for winning success in love and war and trade and husbandry, for bringing harm upon enemies or rivals—charms which a few centuries later will be dressed up in Rigvedic style, stuffed out with imitations of Rigvedic hymns, and published under the name of Atharvaveda, "the lore of the Atharvans," by wizards who claim to belong to the old priestly clans of Atharvan and Angiras. But we have not yet come so far, and as yet all that these people can tell us is a great deal about their black and white magic, in which they are hugely interested, and a fair amount about certain valiant men of olden times who are now worshipped by them as helpful spirits, and a little about some vague spirits who are in the sun and the air and the fire and other places, and are very high and great, but are not interesting at all.

This popular religion seems to be a hopeless one, without ideals and symbols of love and hope. Is there nothing better to be found in this place? Yes, there is a priestly religion also; and if we would know something about it we must listen to the chanting of the priests, the *brahmans* or men of the «holy spirit,» as they are called, who are holding a sacrifice now on behalf of the rich lord who lives in the largest house in the village—a service for which they expect to be paid with a handsome fee of oxen and gold. They are priests by heredity, wise in the knowledge of the ways of the gods; some of them understand how to compose *riks*, or hymns, in the fine speech dear to their order, hymns which are almost sure to win the gods' favour, and all of them know how the sacrifices shall be performed with perfect exactness so that no slip or imperfection may mar their efficacy. Their psalms are called *Rig-veda*, "lore of the verses," and they set themselves to find grace in the ears of the many gods whom these priests worship, sometimes by open praise and sometimes by riddling description of the exploits and nature of the gods. Often they are very fine; but always they are the work of priests, artists in ritual. And if you look heedfully into it you will also mark that these priests are inclined to think that the act of sacrifice, the offering of, say, certain oblations in a particular manner with particular words accompanying them, is in itself potent, quite apart from the psalms which they sing over it, that it has a magic power of its own over the machinery of nature.[1] Really this is no new idea of our Vedic priests; ten thousand years before them their remote forefathers believed it and acted upon it, and if for example they wanted rain they would sprinkle drops of water and utter magic words. Our Vedic priests have now a different kind of symbols, but all the same they still have the notion that ceremony, *rita* as they call it, has a magic potency of its own. Let us mark this well, for we shall see much issuing from it.

Who are the gods to whom these priests offer their prayers and psalms? They are many, and of various kinds. Most of them are taken from the religion of the people, and dressed in new garb according to the imagination of the priest; and a few are priestly inventions altogether. There is Dyaush-pita, the Sky-father, with Prithivi Mata, the Earth-mother; there are Vayu the Wind-spirit, Parjanya the Rain-god, Surya the Sun-god, and other spirits of the sky such as Savita; there is the Dawn-goddess, Ushas. All these are or were originally deified powers of nature: the people, though their imagination created them, have never felt any deep interest in them, and the priests who have taken them into their charge, though they treat them very courteously and sing to them elegant hymns full of figures of speech, have not been able to cover them with the flesh and blood of living personality. Then we have Agni the Fire-god, and Soma the spirit of the intoxicating juice of the soma-plant, which is used to inspire the pious to drunken raptures in certain ceremonies; both of these have acquired a peculiar importance through their association with priestly worship, especially Agni, because he, as bearing to the gods the sacrifices cast into his flames, has become the ideal Priest and divine Paraclete of Heaven. Nevertheless all this hieratic importance has not made them gods in the deeper sense, reigning in the hearts of men. Then we find powers of doubtful origin, Mitra and Varuna and Vishnu and Rudra, and figures of heroic legend, like the warrior Indra and the twin charioteers called Asvinaa and Nasatya. All these, with many others, have their worship in the Rig-veda: the priests sing their praises lustily, and often speak now of one deity, now of another, as being the highest divinity, without the least consistency.

Some savage races believe in a highest god or first divine Being in whom they feel little personal interest. They seldom speak of him, and hardly ever worship him. So it seems to be with Dyaush-pita. The priests speak of him and to him, but only in connection with other gods; he has not a single whole hymn in his honour, and the only definite attribute that attaches to him is that of fatherhood. Yet he has become a great god among other races akin in speech to the Aryans of India: Dyaush-pita is phonetically the same as the Greek [Greek: Zeus pater] and the Latin *Iuppiter*. How comes it then that he is not, and apparently never was, a god in the true sense among the Indian Aryans? Because, I think, his name has always betrayed him. To call a deity "Sky-father" is to label him as a mere abstraction. No mystery, no possibility of human personality, can gather round those two plain prose words. So long as a deity is known by the name of the physical agency that he represents, so long will he be unable to grow into a personal God in India. The priests may sing vociferous psalms to Vayu the Wind-spirit and

Surya the Sun-spirit, and even to their beloved Agni the Fire-god; but sing as much as they will, they never can make the people in general take them to their hearts.

Observe what a different history is that of Zeus among the Greeks—Zeus, Father of Gods and Men, the ideal of kingly majesty and wisdom and goodness. The reason is patent. Ages and ages before the days when the Homeric poets sang, the Greeks had forgotten that Zeus originally meant "sky": it had become to them a personal name of a great spiritual power, which they were free to invest with the noblest ideal of personality. But very likely there is also another reason: I believe that the Olympian Zeus, as modelled by Homer and accepted by following generations, was not the original [Greek: *Zeus patêr*] at all, but a usurper who had robbed the old Sky-father of his throne and of his title as well, that he was at the outset a hero-king who some time after his death was raised to the seat and dignity of the old Sky-father and received likewise his name. This theory explains the old hero-sagas which are connected with Zeus and the strange fact that the Cretans pointed to a spot in their island where they believed Zeus was buried. It explains why legends persistently averred that Zeus expelled his father Kronos from the throne and suppressed the Titan dynasty: on my view, Kronos was the original Father Zeus, and his name of Zeus and rank as chief god were appropriated by a deified hero. How natural such a process was in those days may be seen from the liturgy of Una s on the pyramids at Sakkarah in Egypt.[2] Here Una s is described as rising in heaven after his death as a supreme god, devouring his fathers and mothers, slaughtering the gods, eating their "magical powers," and swallowing their "spirit-souls," so that he thus becomes "the first-born of the first-born gods," omniscient, omnipotent, and eternal, identified with the Osiris, the highest god. Now this Unas was a real historical man; he was the last king of the Fifth Dynasty, and was deified after death, just like any other king of Egypt. The early Egyptians, like many savage tribes, regarded all their kings as gods on earth and paid them formal worship after their death; the later Egyptians, going a step further, worshipped them even in their lifetime as embodiments of the gods.[3] What is said in the liturgy for the deification of Unas is much the same as was said of other kings. The dead king in early Egypt becomes a god, even the greatest of the gods, and he assumes the name of that god[4]; he overcomes the other gods by brute force, he kills and devours them. This is very like what I think was the case with Zeus; the main difference is that in Egypt the *character* of the deified king was merged in that of the old god, and men continued to regard the latter in exactly the same light as before; but among the forefathers of the Greeks the reverse happened in at least one case, that of Zeus, where the character of a hero who had peculiarly fascinated popular imagination partly eclipsed that of the old god whose name and rank he usurped. The reason for this, I suppose, is that even the early Egyptians had already a conservative religion with fixed traditions and a priesthood that forgot nothing,[5] whereas among the forefathers of the Greeks, who were wandering savages, social order and religion were in a very fluid state. However that may be, a deified hero might oust an older god and reign under his name; and this theory explains many difficulties in the legends of Zeus.

As to the Roman Iuppiter, I need not say much about him. Like all the genuine gods of Latium, he never was much more than an abstraction until the Greeks came with their literature and dressed him in the wardrobe of their Zeus.

Coming now to Ushas, the Lady of the Dawn, and looking at her name from the standpoint of comparative philosophy, we see that the word *ushas* is closely connected with the Greek [Greek: heôs] and the Latin *aurora*. But when we read the literature, we are astonished to find that while the Greek Dawn-lady has remained almost always a mere abstraction, the Indian spirit is a lovely, living woman instinct with the richest sensuous charms of the East. Some twenty hymns are addressed to her, and for the most part they are alive with real poetry, with a sense of beauty and gladness and sometimes withal an under-note of sadness for the brief joys of life. But when we look carefully into it we notice a curious thing: all this hymn-singing to Ushas is purely literary and artistic, and there is practically no religion at all at the back of it. A few stories are told of her, but they seem to convince no one, and she certainly has no ritual worship apart from these hymns, which are really poetical essays more than anything else. The priestly poets are thrilled with sincere emotion at the sight of the dawn, and are inspired by it to stately and lively descriptions of its beauties and to touching reflections upon the passing of time and mortal life; but in this scene Ushas herself is hardly more than a model from an artist's studio, in a very Bohemian quarter. More than once on account of her free display of her charms she is compared to a dancing girl, or even a common harlot! Here the imagination is at work which in course of time will populate the Hindu Paradise with a celestial *corps de ballet*, the fair and frail Apsarasas. Our Vedic Ushas is a forerunner of that gay company. A charming person, indeed; but certainly no genuine goddess.

As his name shows, Surya is the spirit of the sun. We hear a good deal about him in the Rig-veda, but the whole of it is merely description of the power of the sun in the order of nature, partly allegorical, and partly literal. He is only a nature-power, not a personal god. The case is not quite so clear with Savita, whose name seems to mean literally "stimulator," "one who stirs up." On the whole it seems most likely that he represents the sun, as the vivifying power in nature, though some[6] think that he was originally an abstraction of the vivifying forces in the world and later became connected with the sun. However this may be, Savita is and remains an impersonal spirit with no human element in his character.

Still more perplexing are the two deities Mitra and Varuna, who are very often associated with one another, and apparently are related. Mitra certainly is an old god: if we go over the mountains to the west and north-west of the country of our Indian Aryans, we shall find their kinsmen in Persia and Bactria worshipping him as a power that maintains the laws of righteousness and guards the sanctity of oaths and engagements, who by means of his watchmen keeps mankind under his observation and with his terrible weapons crushes evil powers. The Indian Aryans tell almost exactly the same tale of their Mitra and his companion Varuna, who perhaps is simply a doublet of Mitra with a different name, which perhaps is due to a variety of worship. But they have more to say of Varuna than of Mitra. In Varuna we have the highest ideal of spirituality that Hindu religion will reach for many centuries. Not only is he described as supreme controller of the order of nature—that is an attribute which these priestly poets ascribe with generous inconsistency to many others of their deities—but he is likewise the omniscient guardian of the moral law and the rule of religion, sternly punishing sin and falsehood with his dreaded noose, but showing mercy to the penitent and graciously communing with the sage who has found favour in his eyes.

But Mitra and Varuna will not enjoy this exalted rank for long. Soon the priests will declare that Mitra rules over the day and Varuna over the night (TS. II. i. 7, 4; VI. iv. 8, 3), and then Varuna will begin to sink in honour. The "noose of Varuna" will come to mean merely the disease of dropsy. His connection with the darkness of the night will cause men to think of him with fear; and in their dread they will forget his ancient attributes of universal righteousness, justice, and mercy, and remember him chiefly as an avenger of guilt. They will banish him to the distant seas, whose rivers he now guides over the earth in his gracious government of nature; and there he will dwell in exile forever, remembered only to be feared. And Mitra will become merely another name for the sun.

What is the origin of this singular couple? And why are they destined to this fall? Neither of these questions can be answered by anything but conjectures. There is no evidence either from Indian or from Iranian religion that Mitra or his double Varuna grew out of the worship of the sun or the sky, although in their worship they were sometimes connected with the sun and the sky. However far backwards we look, we still find them essentially spirits of natural order and moral law, gods in the higher sense of the word. But their character, and especially the character of Varuna, it seems to me, is rather too high to survive the competition of rival cults, such as that of the popular hero Indra and the priests' darling Agni, which tend to engross the interest of worshippers lay and cleric, and to blunt their relish for more spiritual ideals. So Mitra and Varuna become stunted in their growth; and at last comes the fatal time when they are identified with the sky by day and night. This is the final blow. No deity that is plainly limited to any one phase or form of nature in India can be or become a great god; and speedily all their real divinity fades away from Mitra and Varuna, and they shrivel into insignificance.

Next we turn to a spirit of a very different sort, the Fire-god, Agni. The word *agni* is identical with the Latin *ignis*; it means "fire," and nothing else but fire, and this fact is quite sufficient to prevent Agni from becoming a great god. The priests indeed do their best, by fertile fancy and endless repetition of his praises, to lift him to that rank; but even they cannot do it. From the days of the earliest generations of men Fire was a spirit; and the household fire, which cooks the food of the family and receives its simple oblations of clarified butter, is a kindly genius of the home. But with all his usefulness and elfish mystery Fire simply remains fire, and there's an end of it, for the ordinary man. But the priests will not have it so. The chief concern of their lives is with sacrifice, and their deepest interest is in the spirit of the sacrificial fire. All the riches of their imagination and their vocabulary are lavished upon him, his forms and his activities. They have devoted to him about 200 hymns and many occasional verses, in which they dwell with constant delight and ingenious metaphor upon his splendour, his power, his birth from wood, from the two firesticks, from trees of the forest, from stones, or as lightning from the clouds, his kinship with the sun, his dwelling in three abodes (viz. as a rule on earth, in the clouds as lightning, and in the upper heavens as the sun), his place in the homes of men as a holy guest, a friend and a kinsman, his protection of worshippers against evil spirits and malignant sorcerers, and especially his function of conveying the oblation poured into his flames up to the gods. Thus they are led to represent him as the divine Priest, the ideal hierophant, in whom are united the functions of the three chief classes of Rigvedic sacrificial priests, the *hota*, *adhvaryu*, and *brahman*, and hence as an all-knowing sage and seer. If infinite zeal and ingenuity in singing Agni's praises and glorifying his activities can avail to raise him to the rank of a great god, we may expect to find him very near the top. But it is not to be. The priests cannot convince the plain man of Agni's super-godhead, and soon they will fail to convince even themselves. The time will shortly come when they will regard all these gods as little more than puppets whose strings are pulled by the mysterious spirit of the sacrifice.

The priests have another pet deity, Soma. For the sacred rites include the pressing and drinking of the fermented yellow juice of the soma-plant, an acid draught with intoxicating powers, which when mixed with milk and drunk in the priestly rites inspires religious ecstasy. This drinking of the soma-juice is already an ancient and important feature in the worship of our Aryans, as it is also among their kinsmen in Iran; so it is no wonder that the spirit of the sacred plant has been made by the priests into an important deity and celebrated with endless abundance of praise and prayer. As with Agni, Soma's appearance and properties are described with inexhaustible wealth of epithets and metaphors. The poets love to dwell on the mystic powers of this wonderful potion, which can heal sickness of soul and body and inspire gods and men to mighty deeds and holy ecstasy. Most often they tell how the god Indra drank huge potions of it to strengthen himself for his great fight with the dragon Vritra. Most of this worship is of priestly invention; voluminous as its rhetoric is, it makes no great impression on the laity, nor perhaps on the clergy either. Some of the more ingenious of the priests are already beginning to trace an affinity between Soma and the moon. The yellow soma-stalks swell in the water of the pressing-vat, as the yellow moon waxes in the sky; the *soma* has a magical power of stimulation, and the moon sends forth a mystic liquid influence over the vegetation of the earth, and especially over magic plants; the soma is an ambrosia drunk by gods and heroes to inspire them to mighty deeds, and the moon is a bowl of ambrosia which is periodically drunk by the gods and therefore wanes month by month. The next step will soon be taken, and the priests will say that Soma *is* the moon; and literature will then obediently accept this statement, and, gradually forgetting nearly everything that Soma meant to the Rigvedic priests, will use the name Soma merely as a secondary name for Chandra, the moon and its god. A very illuminating process, which shows how a god may utterly change his nature. Now we turn to the hero-gods.

Indra and the Asvina at the beginning came to be worshipped because they were heroes, men who were supposed to have wrought marvellously noble and valiant deeds in dim far-off days, saviours of the afflicted, champions of the right, and who for this reason were worshipped after death, perhaps even before death, as divine beings, and gradually became associated in their legends and the forms of their worship with all kinds of other gods. Times change, gods grow old and fade away, but the remembrance of great deeds lives on in strange wild legends, which, however much they may borrow from other worships and however much they may be obscured by the phantom lights of false fancy, still throw a glimmer of true light back through the darkness of the ages into an immeasurably distant past.

Indra is a mighty giant, tawny of hair and beard and tawny of aspect. The poets tell us that he bears up or stretches out earth and sky, even that he has created heaven and earth. He is a monarch supreme among the gods, the lord of all beings, immeasurable and irresistible of power. He rides in a golden chariot drawn by two tawny horses, or many horses, even as many as eleven hundred, and he bears as his chief weapon the *vajra*, or thunderbolt, sometimes also a bow with arrows, a hook, or a net. Of all drinkers of soma he is the lustiest; he swills many lakes of it, and he eats mightily of the flesh of bulls and buffaloes. To his worshippers he gives abundance of wealth and happiness, and he leads them to victory over hostile tribes of Aryans and the still more dreaded hordes of dark-skins, the Dasas and Dasyus. He guided the princes Yadu and Turvasa across the rivers, he aided Divodasa Atithigva to discomfit the dark-skinned Sambara, he gave to Divodasa's son Sudas the victory over the armies of the ten allied kings beside the river Parushni. Many are the names of the devils and demons that have fallen before him; but most glorious of all his deeds is the conquest of Vritra, the dragon dwelling in a mountain fastness amidst the waters, where Indra, accompanied by the troop of Maruts, or storm-gods, slew the monster with his bolt and set free the waters, or recovered the hidden kine. Our poets sing endless variations on this theme, and sometimes speak of Indra repeating the exploit for the benefit of his worshippers, which is as much as to say that they, or at least some of them, think it an allegory.

In all this maze of savage fancy and priestly invention and wild exaggeration there are some points that stand out clearly. Indra is a god of the people, particularly of the fighting man, a glorified type of the fair-haired, hard-fighting, hard-drinking forefathers of the Indian Aryans and their distant cousins the Hellenes; and therefore he is the champion of their armies in battles. He is not a fiction of hieratic imagination, whom priests regale with hyperbolic flattery qualified only by the lukewarmness of their belief in their own words. He is a living personality in the faith of the people; the priests only invent words to express the people's faith, and perhaps add to the old legends some riddling fancies of their own. Many times they tell us that after conquering Vritra and setting free the waters or the kine Indra created the light, the dawn, or the sun; or they say that he produced them without mentioning any fight with Vritra; sometimes they speak of him as setting free "the kine of the Morning," which means that they understood the cows to signify the light of morning, and it would seem also that they thought that the waters mentioned in the story signified the rain. But why do they speak of these acts as heroic deeds, exploits of a mighty warrior, in the same tone and with the same epic fire as when they sing of Indra's battles in times near to their own, real battles in which their own forefathers, strong in their faith in the god, shattered the armies of hostile Aryan tribes or the fortresses of dark-skinned natives? The personality of Indra and the spirit in which his deeds are recounted remind us of hero-sagas; the allegories which the poets read into them are on the other hand quite in the style of the priest. How can we explain the presence of these two voices? Besides, why should the setting free of the rain or the daylight be a peculiarly heroic attribute of Indra? Other gods are said to do the same things as part of their regular duties: Parjanya, Mitra and Varuna, Dyaus, dispense the rain, others the light.

The explanation is simple. Indra, it seems to me, is a god of just the same sort as Zeus, whose nature and history I have already explained according to my lights. In the far-away past Indra was simply a hero: very likely he was once a chieftain on earth. The story of his great deeds so fascinated the imagination of men that they worshipped his memory and at last raised him to the rank of a chief god. Now they had previously worshipped two very high gods; one of these was Dyaush-pita, the Sky-father, of whom I have spoken before, and another was Tvashta, the All-creator. So some of them, as the Rig-veda proves, declared that Dyaus was the father of Indra, and others appear to have given this honour to Tvashta, while others regarded Tvashta as Indra's grandfather; and some even said that in order to obtain the soma to inspire him to divine deeds Indra killed his father, which of course is just an imaginative way of saying that Indra was made into a god and worshipped in place of the elder god.

The puzzle now is solved. Indra has remained down to the time of the Rig-veda true to his early nature, an epic hero and typical warrior; but he has also borrowed from the old Sky-father the chief attributes of a sky-spirit, especially the giving of rain and the making of light, which the priests of the Rig-veda riddlingly describe as setting free the waters and the cows. He bears the thunderbolt, as does also Zeus; like Zeus, he has got it from the Sky-father, who had likewise a thunderbolt, according to some Rigvedic poets, though others say it was forged for him by Tvash a, his other father. I even venture to think that there is a kernel of heroic legend in the story of the slaying of Vritra; that at bottom it is a tale relating how Indra with a band of brave fellows stormed a mountain hold surrounded by water in which dwelt a wicked chieftain who had carried away the cattle of his people, and that when Indra had risen to the rank of a great god of the sky men added to this plain tale much mythical decoration appropriate to his new quality, turning the comrades of Indra into the storm-gods and interpreting the waters and cows to mean rain and daylight. Since most of us are agreed that stories such as that of Indra defeating Sambara for the benefit of Divodasa refer to real events, it seems unnatural to suppose that the Vritra-legend is a purely imaginary myth. We can thus explain why the ideas of Indra setting free the rain and the light fit in so awkwardly with the heroic element in the legend: for they are merely secondary attributes, borrowed from the myths of other gods and mechanically attached to Indra on his elevation in the pantheon. But we can explain much more. There is a regular cycle of hero-saga connected with Indra which is visible or half-visible at the back of some of the Vedic hymns and of the priestly literature which is destined to follow them.

The truth is that the priests of the Rig-veda on the whole have not quite made up their minds about Indra's merits, and we shall find them a few generations hence equally uncertain. They praise his heroic deeds lustily and admire his power immensely; but they are keenly aware that he is a god with a past, and sometimes they dwell on that. Their favourite method is to relate some of his former questionable deeds in the form of a reproach, and then to turn the story to his credit in some way or another; but as time goes on and the priests think less and less of most of their gods, Indra's character will steadily sink, and in the end we shall find him playing a subordinate part, a debauched king in a sensuous paradise, popularly worshipped as a giver of rain. But this is to anticipate. As yet Indra is to the Rigvedic priests a very great god; but how did he become so? If we read carefully the hymn RV. IV. xviii.[7] we see at the back of it a story somewhat like this. Before he was born, Tvashta, Indra's grandfather, knew that Indra would dispossess him of his sovereignty over the gods, and therefore did his best to prevent his birth (cf. RV. III. xlviii.); but the baby Indra would not be denied, and he forced his way into the light of day through the side of his mother Aditi, who seems to be the same as Mother Earth (cf. *Ved. Stud.*, ii, p. 86), killed his father, and drank Tvash a's soma, by which he obtained divine powers. In v. 12 of this hymn Indra excuses himself by saying that he was in great straits, and that then the soma was brought to him by an eagle. What these straits were is indicated in another hymn (IV. xxvii.), which tells us that he was imprisoned, and escaped on the back of the eagle, which he compelled to carry him; the watchman Krisanu shot an arrow at the bird, but it passed harmlessly through its feathers. Evidently in the story Indra had a hard struggle with rival gods. One poet says (RV. IV. xxx. 3): "Not even all the gods, O Indra, defeated thee, when thou didst lengthen days into nights," which apparently refers also to some miracle like that ascribed to Joshua. Another tradition (MS. I. vi. 12) relates that while Indra and his brother Vivasvan were still unborn they declared their resolve to oust the Adityas, the elder sons of their mother Aditi; so the Adityas tried to kill them when born, and actually slew Vivasvan, but Indra escaped. Another version (TS. II. iv. 13) says that the gods, being afraid of Indra, bound him with fetters before he was born; and at the same time Indra is identified with the Rajanya, or warrior class, as its type and representative.[8] This last point is immensely important, for it really clinches the matter. Not once, but repeatedly, the priestly literature of the generations that will follow immediately after that of the Rig-veda will be found to treat Indra as the type of the warrior order.[9] They will describe an imaginary coronation-ceremony of Indra, ending with these words: «Anointed with this great anointment Indra won all victories, found all the worlds, attained the superiority, pre-eminence, and supremacy over all the gods, and having won the overlordship, the paramount rule, the self rule, the sovereignty, the supreme authority, the kingship, the great kingship, the suzerainty in this world, self-existing, self-ruling, immortal, in yonder world of heaven, having attained all desires he became immortal.»[10] Thus we see that amidst the maze of obscure legends about Indra there are three points which stand out with perfect clearness. They are, firstly, that Indra was a usurper; secondly, that the older gods fought hard but vainly to keep him from supreme divinity, and that in his struggle he killed his father; and thirdly, that he was identified with the warrior class, as opposed to the priestly order, or Brahmans. This antagonism to the Brahmans is brought out very clearly in some versions of the tales of his exploits. More than once the poets of the Rig-veda hint that his slaying of Vritra involved some guilt, the guilt of *brahma-hatya*, or slaughter of a being in whom the *brahma*, or holy spirit, was embodied[11]; and this is explained clearly in a priestly tale (TS. II. v. 2, 1 ff.; cf. SB. I. i. 3, 4, vi. 3, 8), according to which Indra from jealousy killed Tvashta's son Visvarupa, who was chaplain of the gods, and thus he incurred the guilt of *brahma-hatya*. Then Tvash a held a soma-sacrifice; Indra, being excluded from it, broke up the ceremony and himself drank the soma. The soma that was left over Tvash a cast into one of the sacred fires and produced thereby from it the giant Vritra, by whom the whole universe, including Agni and Soma, was enveloped (cf. the later version in Mahabharata, V. viii. f.). By slaying him Indra again became guilty of *brahma-hatya*; and some Rigvedic poets hint that it was the consciousness of this sin which made him flee away after the deed was done.

These bits of saga prove, as effectually as is possible in a case like this, that Indra was originally a warrior-king or chieftain who was deified, perhaps by the priestly tribe of the Angirasas, who claim in some of the hymns to have aided him in his fight with Vritra, and that he thus rose to the first rank in the pantheon, gathering round himself a great cycle of heroic legend based upon those traditions, and only secondarily and by artificial invention becoming associated with the control of the rain and the daylight.

The name Asvina means "The Two Horsemen"; what their other name, Nasatya, signifies nobody has satisfactorily explained. But even with the name Asvina there is a difficulty. They are described usually as riding together in a chariot which is sometimes said to be drawn by horses, and this would suit their name; but more often the poets say that their chariot is drawn by birds, such as eagles or swans, and sometimes even by a buffalo or buffaloes, or by an ass. I do not see how we can escape from this difficulty except by supposing that popular imagination in regard to this matter varied from very early times, but preferred to think of them as having horses. At any rate they are very ancient gods, for the people of Iran also have traditions about them, and in the far-away land of the Mitanni, in the north of Mesopotamia, they are invoked together with Indra, Mitra, and Varuna to sanction treaties. In India the Aryans keep them very busy, for they are more than anything else gods of help. Thrice every day and thrice every night they sally forth on their patrols through earth and heaven, in order to aid the distressed[12]: and the poets tell us the names of many persons whom they have relieved, such as old Chyavana, whom they restored to youth and love, Bhujyu, whom they rescued from drowning in the ocean, Atri, whom they saved from a fiery pit, Vispala, to whom when her leg had been cut off they gave one of iron, and Ghosha, to whom they brought a husband. Many other helpful acts are ascribed to them, and it is very likely that at least some of these stories are more or less true. Another legend relates that they jointly wedded Surya, the daughter of the Sun-god, who chose them from amongst the other gods.[13]

Amidst the medley of saga and facts and poetical imagination which surrounds the Asvina, can we see the outlines of their original character? It is hard to say: opinions must differ. The Aryans of India are inclined to say that they are simply divine kings active in good works; but the priests are perhaps beginning to fancy that they may be embodiments of powers of nature—they are not sure which—and in course of time they will have various theories, partly connected with their rituals. But really all that is certain in the Vedic age about the Asvins is that they are an ancient pair of saviour-gods who ride about in a chariot and render constant services to mankind. We are tempted however to see a likeness between them and the [Greek: Diòs kórô] of the distant Hellenes, the heroes Kastor and Polydeukes, Castor and Pollux, the twin Horsemen who are saviours of afflicted mankind by land and sea. There are difficulties in the way of this theory; but they are not insurmountable, and I believe that the Asvina of India have the same origin as the Twin Horsemen of Greece. At any rate both the pairs are hero-gods, whose divinity has been created by mankind's need for help and admiration for valour. Whether there was any human history at the back of this process we cannot say.

Now we may leave the heroes and consider a god of a very different kind, Vishnu.

The Rig-veda has not very much to say about Vishnu, and what it says is puzzling. The poets figure him as a beneficent young giant, of unknown parentage, with two characteristic attributes: the first of these is his three mystic strides, the second his close association with Indra. Very often they refer to these three strides, sometimes using the verb *vi-kram*, "to step out," sometimes the adjectives *uru-krama*, "widely-stepping," and *uru-gaya*, "wide-going." The three steps carry Vishnu across the three divisions of the universe, in the highest of which is his home, which apparently he shares with Indra (RV. I. xxxii. 20, cliv. 5-6, III. lv. 10; cf. AB. I. i., etc.). Some of them are beginning to imagine that these steps symbolise the passage of the sun through the three divisions of the world, the earth, sky, and upper heaven; certainly this idea will be held by many later scholars, though a few will maintain that it denotes the sun at its rising, at midday, and at its setting. Before long we shall find some priests harping on the same notion in another form, saying that Vishnu's head was cut off by accident and became the sun; and later on we shall see Vishnu bearing as one of his weapons a chakra, or discus, which looks like a figure of the sun. But really all this is an afterthought: in the Veda, and the priestly literature that follows directly upon the Veda, Vishnu is *not* the sun. Nor do we learn what he is very readily from his second leading attribute in the Rig-veda, his association with Indra. Yet it is a very clearly marked trait in his character. Not only do the poets often couple the two gods in prayer and praise, but they often tell us that the one performed his characteristic deeds by the help of the other. They say that Vishnu made his three strides by the power of Indra (VIII. xii. 27), or for the sake of Indra (Val. iv. 3), and even that Indra strode along with Vishnu (VI. lxix. 5, VII. xcix. 6), and on the other hand they tell us often that it was by the aid of Vishnu that Indra overcame Vritra and other malignant foes. "Friend Vishnu, stride out lustily," cries Indra before he can strike down Vritra (IV. xviii. 11).[14] The answer to this riddle I find in the Brahmanas, the priestly literature which is about to follow immediately after the Veda. In plain unequivocal words the Brahmanas tell us again and again that *Vishnu is the sacrifice*.[15] Evidently when they repeat this they are repeating an old hieratic tradition; and it is one which perfectly explains the facts of the case. Vishnu, I conceive, was originally nothing more or less than the embodied spirit of the sacrificial rites. His name seems to be derived from the root *vish*, meaning stimulation or inspiration; and this is exactly what the sacrifice is supposed in priestly theory to do. The sacrifice, accompanied by prayer and praise, is imagined to have a magic power of its own, by which the gods worshipped in it are strengthened to perform their divine functions. One poet says to Indra: "When thy two wandering Bays thou dravest hither, thy praiser laid within thine arms the thunder" (RV. I. lxiii. 2); and still more boldly another says: "Sacrifice, Indra, made thee wax so mighty ... worship helped thy bolt when slaying the dragon" (III. xxxii. 12). So it would be very natural for the priests to conceive this spirit of the sacrificial rites as a personal deity; and this deity, the Brahmanas assure us, is Vishnu. Then the idea of the three strides and the association with Indra would easily grow up in the priestly imagination. The inspiring power of the sacrifice is supposed to pervade the three realms of the universe, earth, sky, and upper heavens; this idea is expressed in the common ritual formula *bhur bhuvas sva* , and is symbolised by three steps taken by the priest in certain ceremonies, which are translated into the language of myth as the three strides of Vishnu.[16] Observe that in the Rig-veda the upper heaven is not the dwelling-place of Vishnu only; Agni the Fire-god, Indra and Soma have their home in it also (RV. I. cliv. 6, IV. xxvi. 6, xxvii. 3-4, V. iii. 3, VIII. lxxxix. 8, IX. lxiii. 27, lxvi. 30, lxviii. 6, lxxvii. 2, lxxxvi. 24, X. i. 3, xi. 4, xcix. 8, cxliv. 4). Later, however, when their adventitious divinity begins to fade away from Agni and Soma, and Indra is allotted a special paradise of his own, this "highest step" will be regarded as peculiar to Vishnu, *Vishno paramam padam.*

As soon as this spirit of sacrifice was thus personified, he at once attached himself to Indra; for Indra is pre-eminently the god of action, and for his activities he needs to be stimulated by sacrifice and praise. As the priests will tell us in plain unvarnished words, "he to whom the Sacrifice comes as portion slays Indra" (AB. I. iv.). Therefore we are told that Vishnu aids Indra in his heroic exploits, that Vishnu takes his strides and presses Soma in order that Indra may be strengthened for his tasks. Now we can see the full meaning of Indra's cry before striking Vritra, "Friend Vishnu, stride out lustily!"; for until the sacrifice has put forth its mystic energy the god cannot strike his blow. We are told also that Vishnu cooks buffaloes and boils milk for Indra,[17] for buffaloes were no doubt anciently offered to Indra. The vivid reality of Indra's character has clothed Vishnu with some of its own flesh and blood; originally a priestly abstraction, he has become through association with Indra a living being, a real god. The blood which has thus been poured into his veins will enable him to live through a critical period of his life, until by combination with another deity he will rise to new and supreme sovereignty. But of that more anon. Meanwhile let us note the significance of this union of Vishnu and Indra in the Veda. Vishnu, the spirit of Sacrifice, is in a sense representative of the Brahman priesthood, and Indra, as I have shown, is commonly regarded as typical of the warrior order. In the Rig-veda Indra is powerless without Vishnu's mystic service, and Vishnu labours to aid Indra in his heroic works for the welfare of men and gods. Surely this is an allegory, though the priests may so far be only dimly conscious of its full meaning—an allegory bodying forth the priestly ideal of the reign of righteousness, in which the King is strong by the mystic power of the Priest, and the Priest lives for the service of the King.

There is another god who is destined to become in future ages Vishnu's chief rival—Rudra, "The Tawny," or Siva, "The Gracious." He belongs to the realm of popular superstition, a spiteful demon ever ready to smite men and cattle with disease, but likewise dispensing healing balms and medicines to those that win his favour. The Rigvedic priests as yet do not take much interest in him, and for the most part they leave him to their somewhat despised kinsmen the Atharvans, who do a thriving trade in hymns and spells to secure the common folk against his wrath.

There are many more gods, godlings, and spirits in the Vedic religion; but we must pass over them. We have seen enough, I hope, to give us a fair idea of the nature and value of that religion in general. What then is its value?

The Rigveda is essentially a priestly book; but it is not entirely a priestly book. Much of the thought to which it gives utterance is popular in origin and sentiment, and is by no means of the lowest order. On this groundwork the priests have built up a system of hieratic thought and ritual of their own, in which there is much that deserves a certain respect. There is a good deal of fine poetry in it. There is also in it some idea of a law of righteousness: in spite of much wild and unmoral myth and fancy, its gods for the most part are not capricious demons but spirits who act in accordance with established laws, majestic and wise beings in whom are embodied the highest ideals to which men have risen as yet. Moreover, the priests in the later books have given us some mystic hymns containing vigorous and pregnant speculations on the deepest questions of existence, speculations which are indeed fanciful and unscientific, but which nevertheless have in them the germs of the powerful idealism that is destined to arise in centuries to come. On the other hand, the priests have cast their system in the mould of ritualism. Ritual, ceremony, sacrifice, professional benefit—these are their predominant interests. The priestly ceremonies are conceived to possess a magical power of their own; and the fixed laws of ritual by which these ceremonies are regulated tend to eclipse, and finally even to swallow up, the laws of moral righteousness under which the gods live. A few generations more, and the priesthood will frankly announce its ritual to be the supreme law of the universe. Meanwhile they are becoming more and more indifferent to the personalities of the gods, when they have preserved any; they are quite ready to ascribe attributes of one deity to another, even attributes of nominal supremacy, with unscrupulous inconsistency and dubious sincerity; for the personalities of the different gods are beginning to fade away in their eyes, and in their mind is arising the conception of a single universal Godhead.

Endnotes

1. Cf. e.g. RV. III. xxxii. 12.
2. Sir E. A. W. Budge, *Literature of the Ancient Egyptians*, p. 21 ff., and *Gods of the Egyptians*, i, pp. 32 f., 43.
3. Erman, *Handbook of Egyptian Religion*, p. 37 f.
4. Budge, *Lit. of the Egyptians*, p. 21; Erman, *ut supra*, p. 37 f.
5. It is even possible that in one case, that of Osiris, a hero in Egypt may have eclipsed by his personality the god whom he ousted. See Sir J. W. Frazer's *Adonis, Attis, Osiris*, ii, p. 200, and Sir W. Ridgeway's *Dramas and Dramatic Dances, etc.*, p. 94 ff.
6. See Oldenberg, *Religion des Veda*, p. 64 f.
7. I follow in the interpretation of this hymn E. Sieg, *Die Sagenstoffe des gveda*, i. p. 76 ff. Cf. on the subject *Ved. Stud.*, i. p. 211, ii. pp. 42-54. Charpentier, *Die Suparnasage*, takes a somewhat different view of RV. IV. xxvi.-xxvii., which, however, does not convince me; I rather suspect that RV. IV. xxvi. 1 and 4, with their mention of Manu, to whom the s ma was brought, are echoes of an ancient and true tradition that Indra was once a mortal.
8. The other legend in MS. II. i. 12, that Aditi bound the unborn Indra with an iron fetter, with which he was born, and of which he was able to rid himself by means of a sacrifice, is probably later.
9. E.g. AB. VII. xxxi., VIII. xii. Cf. BA. Up. I. iv. 11-13.

10. AB. VIII. xiv. (Keith's translation).

11. Cf. Sayana on RV. I. xciii. 5.

12. Cf. *Ved. Studien*, ii. p. 31, RV. I. xxxiv. 2.

13. Cf. *Ved. Studien*, i. p. 14 ff.

14. A later and distorted version of this myth appears in AB. VI. xv.

15. E.g. MS. 1. iv. 14, SB. I. i. 1, 2, 13, TB. I. ii. 5, 1, AB. I. xv., KB. IV. ii., XVIII. viii., xiv.

16. SB. I. ix. 3, 8-11. Cf. the three steps of the Amesha-spentas from the earth to the sun, imitated in the Avestic ritual (Avesta, transl. Darmesteter, I. 401).

17. SB. I. ix. 3, 8-11. Cf. the three steps of the Amesha-spentas from the earth to the sun, imitated in the Avestic ritual (Avesta, transl. Darmesteter, I. 401).

CHAPTER 2

THE AGE OF THE BRAHMANAS
AND UPANISHADS

Centuries have passed since the hymns of the Rig-veda were composed. The Aryans have now crossed the fateful ridge on the east of their former settlements, and have spread themselves over the lands of Northern Hindostan around the upper basins of the Ganges and Jamna, reaching eastward as far as Bihar and southward down to the Vindhya Mountains, and in the course of their growth they have absorbed not a little of the blood of the dark-skinned natives. The old organisation of society by tribes has come to an end, though the names of many ancient tribes are still heard; the Aryans are now divided laterally by the principle of what we call "caste," which is based upon a combination of religious and professional distinctions, and vertically by the rule of kings, while a few oligarchic governments still survive to remind them of Vedic days. In these kingdoms the old tribes are beginning to be fused together; from these combinations new States are arising, warring with one another, constantly waxing and waning. Society is ruled politically by kings, spiritually by Brahmans. With the rise of the kingdom an Established Church has come into existence, and the Brahman priesthood works out its principles to the bitterest end of logic.

The Brahmans are now, more than they ever were before, a close corporation of race, religion, and profession, a religious fraternity in the strict sense of the words. While other classes of the Aryans have mixed their blood to a greater or less degree with that of the natives, the Brahmans have preserved much of the pure Aryan strain. They, moreover, have maintained the knowledge of the ancient Vedic language in which the sacred hymns of their forefathers were composed, of the traditions associated with them, and of the priestly lore of Vedic ritual. Proud of this heritage and resolved to maintain it undiminished, they have knitted themselves into a close spiritual and intellectual aristocracy, which stands fast like a lighthouse amidst the darkness and storms of political changes. They employ all the arts of the priest, the thinker, the statesman, and even the magician to preserve their primacy; and around them the manifold variety of the other castes, in all their divisions and subdivisions, groups itself to make up the multi-coloured web of Indian life.

In course of time this priesthood will spread out octopus-like tentacles over the whole of India. Becoming all things to all men, it will find a place in its pantheon for all gods and all ideas, baptising them by orthodox names or justifying them by ingenious fictions. It will send forth apostles and colonies even to the furthermost regions of the distant South, which, alien in blood and in tradition, will nevertheless accept them and surrender its best intellect to their control. It will even admit into the lower ranks of its own body men of foreign birth by means of legal fictions, in order to maintain its control of religion. Though itself splitting up into scores of divisions varying in purity of blood and tradition, it will still as a whole maintain its position as against all other classes of society. That the Brahman is the Deity on earth, and other classes shall accept this dogma and agree to take their rank in accordance with it, will become the principle holding together a vast agglomeration of utterly diverse elements within the elastic bounds of Catholic Brahmanism.

But as yet this condition of things has not arrived. The Brahmans are still comparatively pure in blood and homogeneous in doctrine, and they have as yet sent forth no colonies south of the Vindhya. They are established in the lands of the Ganges and Jamna as far to the east as Benares, and they look with some contempt on their kinsmen in the western country that they have left behind. They are busily employed in working out to logical conclusions the ideas and principles of their Rigvedic forefathers. They have now three Vedas; for to the old Rig-veda they have added a Yajur-veda for the use of the sacrificant orders of priests and a Sama-veda or hymnal containing Rigvedic hymns arranged for the chanting of choristers. The result of these labours is that they have created a vast and intricate system of sacrificial ritual, perhaps the most colossal of its kind that the world has ever seen or ever will see. What is still more remarkable, the logical result of this immense development of ritualism is that the priesthood in theory is practically atheistic, while on the other hand a certain number of its members have arrived at a philosophy of complete idealism which is beginning to turn its back upon ritualism.

The atheist is not so much the man who denies the existence of any god as the man to whom God is not God, who looks upon the Deity as subordinate to powers void of holiness and nobility, the man who will not see in God the highest force in the world of nature and in the realm of the spirit. In this sense the Brahmans are thorough atheists. According to them, the universe with all that is in it—gods, men, and lower things—is created and governed by an iron law of soulless natural necessity. It has arisen by emanation from a cosmic Principle, Prajapati, "the Lord of Creatures," an impersonal being who shows no trace of moral purpose in his activity. Prajapati himself is not absolutely the first in the course of nature. The Brahmanas, the priestly books composed in this period to expound the rules and mystic significance of the Brahmanic ceremonies, give us varying accounts of his origin, some of them saying that he arose through one or more intermediate stages from non-existence (TB. II. ii. 9, 1-10, SB. VI. i. 1, 1-5), others deriving him indirectly from the primitive waters (SB. XI. i. 6, 1), others tracing his origin back to the still more impersonal and abstract Brahma (Samav. B. I. 1-3, Gop. B. I. i. 4). All these are attempts to express in the form of myth the idea of an impersonal Principle of Creation as arising from a still more abstract first principle. We have seen

the poets of the Rig-veda gradually moving towards the idea
of a unity of godhead; in Prajapati this goal is attained, but
unfortunately it is attained by sacrificing almost all that is truly
divine in godhead. The conception of Prajapati that we find in
the Brahmanas is also expressed in some of the latest hymns of
the Rig-veda. Among these is the famous Purusha-sukta (RV. X.
90), which throws a peculiar light on the character of Prajapati.
It is in praise of a primitive Purusha or Man, who is, of course,
the same as Prajapati; in some mysterious manner this Purusha is
sacrificed, and from the various parts of his body arise the various
parts of the world. The idea conveyed by this is that the universe
came into existence by the operation of the mystic laws revealed
in the Brahmanic rituals, and is maintained in its natural order
by the same means. The Brahmanas do not indeed often assert on
their own authority that Prajapati was himself sacrificed in order
to produce the world, and in fact they usually give other accounts
of the creation; but as their authors live in a rarefied atmosphere
of mystical allegory in which fact and fancy are completely
confused with one another and consistency ceases to have any
meaning, none of them would have difficulty in accepting the
Rigvedic statement that he was sacrificed. Hence they tell us on
the one hand that Prajapati has created the world from a blind
will for generation or increase, producing from each of his limbs
some class of beings corresponding to it (e.g. MS. IV. vi. 3), or
copulating with the earth, atmosphere, sky, and speech (SB. VI.
i. 2, 1), or that he brought it into existence indirectly by entering

with the Triple Science or mystic lore of the three Vedas into the primeval waters and thence forming an egg from which was hatched the personal Demiurge Brahma, who actually created the world (SB. VI. i. 1, 10); and on the other hand they relate that he created sacrifice and performed it, making of himself a victim in order that the gods, his offspring, might perform the rites for their own benefit, forming an image of himself to be the sacrifice, by which he redeemed himself from the gods (SB. XI. i. 8, 2-4; cf. AB. VII. 19, KB. XIII. 1, SB. III. ii. 1, 11), and that after creation he ascended to heaven (SB. X. ii. 2, 1). The thought that lies underneath these bewildering flights of fancy is one of mystic pantheism: all created existence has arisen by emanation from the one Creative Principle, Prajapati, and in essence is one with Prajapati; Prajapati is an impersonal being, a creative force, in which are embodied the laws of Brahmanic ritual, which acts only in these laws, and which is above the moral influences that affect humanity; and the whole of created nature, animate and inanimate, is controlled in every process of its being by these laws, and by the priest who possesses the knowledge of them. Thus there lies a profound significance in the title of "gods on earth" which the Brahmans have assumed.

When we speak of sacrifice in India, we must clear our minds of the ideas which we have formed from reading the Bible. The Mosaic conception of sacrifice was that of a religious ceremony denoting a moral relation between a personal God and His worshippers: in the sin-offerings and trespass-offerings was symbolised a reconciliation between man and his God who was angered by man's conscious or unconscious breach of the laws which had been imposed upon him for his spiritual welfare, while meat-offerings and peace-offerings typified the worshipper's sense of gratitude for the Divine love and wisdom that guarded him. Of such relations there is to be found in the Brahmanas no trace. If we may use a modern figure of speech, they conceive the universe of gods, men, and lower creatures as a single immense electric battery, and the sacrifice as a process of charging this battery with ever fresh electricity. The sacrifice is a process, at once material and mystic, which preserves the order of nature as established by the prototypic sacrifice performed by Prajapati. The gods became divine and immortal through sacrifice (TS. VI. iii. 4, 7, VI. iii. 10, 2, VII. iv. 2, 1, SB. I. vi. 2, 1, MS. III. ix. 4, AB. VI. i. 1, etc.); and they live on the gifts of earth, as mankind lives on the gifts of heaven (TS. III. ii. 9, 7, SB. I. ii. 5, 24). The sacrifice is thus the life-principle, the soul, of all gods and all beings (SB. VIII. vi. 1, 10, IX. iii. 2, 7, XIV. iii. 2, 1); or, what amounts to the same thing, the Triple Science or the knowledge of the ceremonies of the Three Vedas is their essence (SB. X. iv. 2, 21). As Prajapati created the primeval sacrifice, and as the gods by following this rule obtained their divinity, so man should seek to follow their example and by means of sacrifice rise to godhead and immortality. As one Brahmana puts it, the sacrifice leads the way to heaven; it is followed by the *dakshina*, or fee paid by the sacrificer to the sacrificant priests, which of course materially strengthens the efficacy of the sacrifice; and third comes the sacrificer, holding fast to the *dakshina*. This ascent of heaven is symbolised in the ceremony called *durohana*, or "hard mounting" (AB. IV. 20, 21, KB. XXV. 7), and it is ensured by the rite of *diksha*, or consecration, in which the sacrificer is symbolically represented as passing through a new conception, gestation, and birth, by which he is supposed to obtain two bodies. One of these bodies is immortal and spiritual; the other is mortal and material, and is assigned as a victim to all the gods. He then ransoms his material body from the obligation of being sacrificed, as did Prajapati, and thus ranks literally as a "god on earth," with the certainty of becoming in due course a god in heaven.

When the student on reading the Brahmanas finds them full of interminable ceremonial rules with equally interminable commentaries interpreting them by wildest analogies as symbolical of details of myths or of laws of nature and hence as conferring mystic powers, besides all kinds of myths, some forcibly dragged into the interpretation of the ritual because of some imaginary point of resemblance, others invented or recast on purpose to justify some detail of ceremony, and when moreover he observes that many of these myths and some of the rites are brutally and filthily obscene, and that hardly any of them show the least moral feeling, he may be excused for thinking the Brahmanas to be the work of madmen. But there is some method in their madness. However strangely they may express them, they have definite and strictly logical ideas about the sacrificial ritual and its cosmic function. It is more difficult to defend them against the charge of want of morality. It must be admitted that their supreme Being, Prajapati, is in the main lines of his character utterly impersonal, and where incidentally he shows any human feelings they are as a rule far from creditable to him. He created the universe from mechanical instinct or blind desire, and committed or tried to commit incest with his daughter (the accounts are various). He has begotten both the gods and the demons, *devas* and *asuras*, who are constantly at war with one another. The gods, who are embodiments of "truth" (that is to say, correct knowledge of the law of ritual), have been often in great danger of being overwhelmed by the demons, who embody "untruth," and they have been saved by Prajapati; but he has done this not from any sense of right, but merely from blind will or favour, for he can hardly distinguish one party from the other. The gods themselves, in spite of being of "truth," are sadly frail. Dozens of myths charge them with falsehood, hatred, lust, greed, and jealousy, and only the stress of the danger threatening them from their adversaries the demons has induced them to organise themselves into an ordered kingdom under the sovereignty of Indra, who has been anointed by Prajapati. True, many of the offensive features in this mythology and ritual are survivals from a very ancient past, a pre-historic time in which morals were conspicuously absent from religion; the priesthood has forgotten very little, and as a rule has only added new rituals and new interpretations to this legacy from the days of old. Nevertheless it must be confessed that there is a tone of ritualistic professionalism in the Brahmanas that is unpleasing; the priesthood are consciously superior to nature, God, and morals by virtue of their "Triple Science," and they constantly emphasise this claim. It is difficult for us to realise that these are the same men who have created the Brahmanic culture of India, which, however we may criticise it from the Western point of view, is essentially a gentle life, a field in which moral feeling and intellectual effort have born abundance of goodly fruit. Yet if we look more closely we shall see that even these ritualists, besotted as they may seem to be with their orgies of priestcraft, are not wholly untouched by the better spirit of their race. Extremes of sanctity, whether it be ritualistic or anti-ritualistic sanctity, always tend in India—and in other countries as well—to produce super men. And if our priesthood in the Brahmanas feel themselves in the pride of spiritual power lifted above the rules of moral law, they are not in practice indifferent to it. Their lives are for the most part gentle and good. Though "truth" in the Brahmanas usually means only accordance with the ritual and mystic teachings of the Triple Science, it sometimes signifies even there veracity and honesty also. Truthfulness in speech is the hall-mark of the Brahman, says Haridrumata Gautama to Satyakama Jabala (Chhand. Up. IV. iv. 5); and even in the Brahmanas a lie is sometimes a sin. If conservatism compels the priests to keep obscene old practices in their rituals, they are not always satisfied with them, and voices begin to be heard pleading that these rites are really obsolete. In short, a moral sense is beginning to arise among them.

Now the moral law, in order that it may be feared, needs to be embodied in the personality of a god. Most of their gods inspire no fear at all in the souls of the Brahmans; but there is one of whom they have a dread, which is all the greater for being illogical. Prajapati is a vast impersonality, too remote and abstract to inspire the soul with either fear or love. The other gods—Indra, Agni, Soma, Varuna, Vishnu, and the rest—are his offspring, and are moved like puppets by the machinery of the ritual of sacrifice created by him. However much they may seem to differ one from another in their attributes and personalities, they are in essence one and negligible in the eyes of the master of the ritual lore. In the beginning, say the Brahmanas, all the gods (except Prajapati, of course) were alike, and all were mortal; then they performed sacrifices and thereby became immortal, each with his peculiar attributes of divinity.[1] Thus at bottom they are all the same thing, merely phases of the universal godhead, waves stirred up by the current of the cosmic sacrifice. They have no terrors for the priesthood. But there is one deity who obstinately refuses to accommodate himself to this convenient point of view, and that is Rudra, or Siva. By rights and logically he ought to fall into rank with the rest of the gods; but there is a crossgrained element in his nature which keeps him out. As we have seen, he comes from a different source: in origin he was a demon, a power of terror, whose realm of worship lay apart from that of the gods of higher class, and now, although it has extended into the domains of orthodox religion, an atmosphere of dread still broods over it.[2] Rudra wields all his ancient terrors over a much widened area. The priests have assigned him a regular place in their liturgies, and fully recognise him in his several phases as Bhava, Sarva, Ugra, Maha-deva or the Great God, Rudra, Isana or the Lord, and Asani or the Thunderbolt (KB. VI. 2-9). Armed with his terrors, he is fit to be employed in the service of conscience. Hence a myth has arisen that in order to punish Prajapati for his incest with his daughter the gods created Bhuta-pati (who is Pasu-pati or Rudra under a new name), who stabbed him. The rest of the myth is as immaterial to our purpose as it is unsavoury; what is important is that the conscience of the Brahmans was beginning to feel slight qualms at the uncleanness of some of their old myths and to look towards Rudra as in some degree an avenger of sin. In this is implied an immense moral advance. Henceforth there will be a gradual ennoblement of one of the phases of the god's character. Many of the best minds among the Brahmans will find their imaginations stirred and their consciences moved by contemplation of him. To them he will be no more a mere demon of the mountain and the wild. His destructive wrath they will interpret as symbolising the everlasting process of death-in-life which is the keynote of nature; in his wild dances they will see imaged forth the everlasting throb of cosmic existence; to his terrors they will find a reverse of infinite love and grace. The horrors of Rudra the deadly are the mantle of Siva the gracious. Thus, while the god's character in its lower phases remains the same as before, claiming the worship of the basest classes of mankind, and nowise rising to a higher level, it develops powerfully and fruitfully in one aspect which attracts grave and earnest imaginations. The Muni, the contemplative ascetic, penetrates in meditation through the terrors of Siva's outward form to the god's inward love and wisdom, and beholds in him his own divine prototype. And so Siva comes to be figured in this nobler aspect as the divine Muni, the supreme saint and sage.

While the worship of Siva is slowly making its way into the heart of Brahmanic ritualism, another movement is at work which is gradually drawing many of the keenest intellects among the Brahmans away from the study of ritual towards an idealistic philosophy which views all ritual with indifference. Its literature is the Upanishads.

The passing of the Rigvedic age has left to the Brahmans a doctrinal legacy, which may be thus restated: a single divine principle through a prototypic sacrifice has given birth to the universe, and all the processes of cosmic nature are controlled by sacrifices founded upon that primeval sacrifice. In short, the ritual symbolises and in a sense actually *is* the whole cosmic process. The ritual implies both the knowledge of the law of sacrifice and the proper practice of that law, *both understanding and works*. This is the standpoint of the orthodox ritualist. But there has also arisen a new school among the Brahmans, that of the Aupanishadas, which has laid down for its first doctrine that *works are for the sake of understanding*, that the practice of ritual is of value only as a help to the mystic knowledge of the All. But here they have not halted; they have gone a further step, and declared that *knowledge once attained, works become needless.* Some even venture to hint that perhaps the highest knowledge is not to be reached through works at all. And the knowledge that the Aupanishadas seek is of Brahma, and *is* Brahma.

The word *brahma* is a neuter noun, and in the Rig-veda it means something that can only be fully translated by a long circumlocution. It may be rendered as "the power of ritual devotion"; that is to say, it denotes the mystic or magic force which is put forth by the poet-priest of the Rig-veda when he performs the rites of sacrifice with appropriate chanting of hymns—in short, ritual magic. This mystic force the Rigvedic poets have represented in personal form as the god Brihaspati, in much the same way as they embodied the spirit of the sacrifice in Vishnu. Their successors, the orthodox ritualists of the Brahmanas, have not made much use of this term; but sometimes they speak of Brahma as an abstract first principle, the highest and ultimate source of all being, even of Prajapati (Samav. B. I. 1, Gop. B. I. i. 4); and when they speak of Brahma they think of him not as a power connected with religious ceremony but as a supremely transcendent and absolutely unqualified and impersonal First Existence. But the school of the Aupanishadas has gone further. Seeking through works mystic knowledge as the highest reality, they see in Brahma the perfect knowledge. To them the absolute First Existence is also transcendently full and unqualified Thought. As knowledge is power, the perfect Power is perfect Knowledge.

Brahma then is absolute knowledge; and all that exists is really Brahma, one and indivisible in essence, but presenting itself illusively to the finite consciousness as a world of plurality, of most manifold subjects and objects of thought. The highest wisdom, the greatest of all secrets, is to know this truth, to realise with full consciousness that there exists only the One, Brahma, the infinite Idea; and the sage of the Upanishads is he who has attained this knowledge, understanding that he himself, as individual subject of thought, is really identical with the universal Brahma. He has realised that he is one with the Infinite Thought, he has raised himself to the mystic heights of transcendental Being and Knowledge, immeasurably far above nature and the gods. He knows all things at their fountain-head, and life can nevermore bring harm to him; in his knowledge he has salvation, and death will lead him to complete union with Brahma.

The Aupanishadas have thus advanced from the pantheism of the orthodox ritualists to a transcendental idealism. The process has been gradual. It was only by degrees that they reached the idea of salvation in knowledge, the knowledge that is union with Brahma; and it was likewise only through slow stages that they were able to conceive of Brahma in itself. Many passages in the Upanishads are full of struggles to represent Brahma by symbols or forms perceptible to the sense, such as ether, breath, the sun, etc. Priests endeavoured to advance through ritual works to the ideas which these works are supposed to symbolise: the ritual is the training-ground for the higher knowledge, the leading-strings for infant philosophy. Gradually men become capable of thinking without the help of these symbols: philosophy grows to manhood, and looks with a certain contempt upon those supports of its infancy.

The nature of Brahma as conceived in the Upanishads is a subject on which endless controversies have raged, and we need not add to them. Besides, the Upanishads themselves are not strictly consistent on this point, or on others, for that matter; for they are not a single homogeneous system of philosophy, but a number of speculations, from often varying standpoints, and they are frequently inconsistent. But there are some ideas which are more or less present in all of them. They regard Brahma as absolute and infinite Thought and Being at once, and as such it is one with the consciousness, soul or self, of the individual when the latter rids himself of the illusion of a manifold universe and realises his unity with Brahma. Moreover, Brahma is bliss—the joy of wholly perfect and self-satisfied thought and being. Since Brahma as universal Soul is really identical with each individual soul or *atma*, and vice versa, it follows that each individual soul contains within itself, *qua* Brahma, the whole of existence, nature, gods, mankind, and all other beings; it creates them all, and all depend upon it. Our Aupanishadas are thoroughgoing idealists.

Another new idea also appears for the first time in the early Upanishads, and one that henceforth will wield enormous influence in all Indian thought. This is the theory of *karma* and *samsara*, rebirth of the soul in accordance with the nature of its previous works. Before the Upanishads we find no evidence of this doctrine: the nearest approach to it is in some passages of the Brahmanas which speak of sinful men dying again in the next world as a punishment for their guilt. But in the Upanishads the doctrine appears full-fledged, and it is fraught with consequences of immense importance. Samsara means literally a "wandering to and fro," that is, the cycle of births through which each soul must everlastingly pass from infinite time, and Karma means the "acts" of each soul. Each work or act performed by a living being is of a certain degree of righteousness or unrighteousness, and it is requited by a future experience of corresponding pleasure or pain. So every birth and ultimately every experience of a soul is determined by the righteousness of its previous acts; and there is no release for the soul from this endless chain of causes and effects unless it can find some supernatural way of deliverance. The Aupanishadas point to what they believe to be the only way: it is the Brahma knowledge of the enlightened sage, which releases his soul from the chain of natural causation and raises him to everlasting union with Brahma.

The teaching of the Upanishads has had two very different practical results. On the one hand, it has moved many earnest thinkers to cast off the ties of the world and to wander about as homeless beggars, living on alms and meditating and discoursing upon the teachings of the Upanishads, while they await the coming of death to release their souls from the prison of the flesh and bring it to complete and eternal union with Brahma. These wandering ascetics—*sannyasis, bhikshus,* or *parivrajakas* they are called—form a class by themselves, which is destined to have an immense influence in moulding the future thought of India. The teaching of Brahmanism is beginning to recognise them, too. It has already divided the life of the orthodox man into three stages, or *asramas,* studentship, the condition of the married householder, and thirdly the life of the hermit, or *vanaprastha,* to which the householder should retire after he has left a son to maintain his household; and now it is beginning to add to these as fourth stage the life of the homeless ascetic awaiting death and release. But this arrangement is for the most part a fiction, devised in order to keep the beggar-philosophers within the scheme of Brahmanic life; in reality they themselves recognise no such law.

The other current among the Aupanishadas is flowing in a very different direction. We have seen how the worship of Rudra-Siva has grown since the old Rigvedic days, and how some souls have been able to see amidst the terrors of the god a power of love and wisdom that satisfies their deepest hopes and longings, as none of the orthodox rituals can do. A new feeling, the spirit of religious devotion, *bhakti* as it is called, is arising among them. To them—and they number many Brahmans as well as men of other orders—Siva has thus become the highest object of worship, Isvara or "the Lord"; and having thus enthroned him as supreme in their hearts, they are endeavouring to find for him a corresponding place in their intellects. To this end they claim that Siva as Isvara is the highest of all forms of existence; and this doctrine is growing and finding much favour. Among the Aupanishadas there are many who reconcile it with the teaching of the Upanishads by identifying Siva with Brahma. Thus a new light begins to flicker here and there in the Upanishads as the conception of Siva, a personal god wielding free grace, colours the pale whiteness of the impersonal Brahma; and at last in the Svetasvatara, which though rather late in date is not the least important of the Upanishads, this theistic movement boldly proclaims itself: the supreme Brahma, identified with Siva, is definitely contrasted with the individual soul as divine to human, giver of grace to receiver of grace. Later Upanishads will take up this strain, in honour of Siva and other gods, and finally they will end as mere tracts of this or that theistic church.

Yet another current is now beginning to stir men's minds, and it is one that is also destined to a great future. It starts from Krishna.

The teaching of the Upanishads, that all being is the One Brahma and that Brahma is the same as the individual soul, has busied many men, not only Brahmans but also Kshatriyas, noblemen of the warrior order. Some even say that it arose among the Kshatriyas; and at any rate it is likely that they, being less obsessed with the forms of ritual than the Brahmans and therefore able to think more directly and clearly, have helped the Brahmans in their discussions to clear their minds of ritual symbolism, and to realise more definitely the philosophic ideas which hitherto they had seen only dimly typified in their ceremonies.

Krishna was one of these Kshatriyas. He belonged to the Satvata or Vrishni tribe, living in or near the ancient city of Mathura. Sometimes in early writings he is styled Krishna Devakiputra, Krishna Devaki's son, because his mother's name was Devaki; sometimes again he is called Krishna Vasudeva, or simply Vasudeva, which is a patronymic said to be derived from the name of his father Vasudeva. In later times we shall find a whole cycle of legend gathering round him, in which doubtless there is a kernel of fact. Omitting the miraculous elements in these tales, we may say that the outline of the Krishna-legend is as follows: Krishna's father Vasudeva and his mother Devaki were grievously wronged by Devaki's cousin Kamsa, who usurped the royal power in Mathura and endeavoured to slay Krishna in his infancy; but the child escaped, and on growing to manhood killed Kamsa. But Kamsa had made alliance with Jarasandha king of Magadha, who now threatened Krishna; so Krishna prudently retired from Mathura and led a colony of his tribesmen to Dvaraka, on the western coast in Kathiawar, where he founded a new State. There seems to be no valid reason for doubting these statements. Sober history does not reject a tale because it is embroidered with myth and fiction.

Now this man Krishna in the midst of his stirring life of war and government found time and taste also for the things that are of the spirit. He talked with men learned in the Upanishads about Brahma and the soul and the worship of God; and apparently he set up a little Established Church of his own, in which was combined something of the idealism of the Upanishads with the worship of a supreme God of grace and perhaps too a kind of religious discipline, about which we shall say more later on. It must be confessed that we know sadly little about his actual doctrine from first hand. All that we hear about it is a short chapter in the Chhandogya Upanishad (iii. 17), where the Brahman Ghora Angirasa gives a sermon to Krishna, in which he compares the phases of human life to stages in the *diksha* or ceremony of consecration, and the moral virtues that should accompany them to the *dakshina* or honorarium paid to the officiating priests, and he concludes by exhorting his hearer to realise that the Brahma is imperishable, unfailing, and spiritual, and quoting two verses from the Rig-veda speaking of the Sun as typifying the supreme bliss to which the enlightened soul arises. This does not tell us very much, and moreover we should remember that here our author, being an Aupanishada, is more interested in what Ghora preached to Krishna than in what Krishna accepted from Ghora's teaching. But we shall find centuries later in the Bhagavad-gita, the greatest textbook of the religion of Krishna, some distant echoes of this paragraph of the Chhandogya.

The beginnings of the religion of Krishna are thus very uncertain. But as we travel down the ages we find it growing and spreading. We see Krishna himself regarded as a half-divine hero and teacher, and worshipped under the name of *Bhagavan*, "the Lord," in association with other half-divine heroes. We see him becoming identified with old gods, and finally rising to the rank of the Supreme Deity whose worship he had himself taught in his lifetime, the Brahma of the philosophers and the Most High God of the theists. As has happened many a time, the teacher has become the God of his Church.

Endnotes

1. For the original mortality of the gods see TS. VII. iv. 2, 1, SB. X. iv. 33 f., XI. i. 2, 12, ii. 3, 6; for their primitive non-differentiation, TS. VI. vi. 8, 2, SB. IV. v. 4, 1-4.

2. Cf. e.g. KB. III. 4 & 6, VI. 2-9, and Ap. SS. VI. xiv. 11-13.

CHAPTER 3

THE EPICS, AND LATER

I. VISHNU-KRISHNA

We now enter upon an age in which the old gods, Indra and Brahma, retire to the background, while Vishnu and Siva stand in the forefront of the stage.

The Hindus are of the same opinion as the Latin poet: *ferrea nunc aetas agitur*. We are now living in an Iron Age, according to them; and it began in the year 3102 B.C., shortly after the great war described in the Mahabharata. The date 3102, I need hardly remark, is of no historical value, being based merely upon the theories of comparatively late astronomers; but the statement as a whole is important. The Great War marks an epoch. It came at the end of what may be called the pre-historic period, and was followed by a new age. To be strictly correct, we must say that the age which followed the Great War was not new in the sense that it introduced any startling novelties that had been unknown previously; but it was new in the sense that after the Great War India speedily became the India that we know from historical records. A certain fusion of different races, cultures, and ideals had to take place in order that the peculiar civilisation of India might unfold itself; and this fusion was accomplished about the time of the Great War, and partly no doubt by means of the Great War, some ten centuries before the Christian era.

The story of the Great War is told with a wild profusion of mythical and legendary colouring in the Mahabharata, an epic the name of which means literally "The Great Tale of the Bharata Clan." It relates how the blind old King Dhritarashtra of Hastinapura had a hundred sons, known as the Kuru or Kaurava princes, the eldest of whom was Duryodhana, and Dhritarashtra's brother Pandu had five sons, the Pandava brethren; how the Pandavas were ousted by the Kauravas from the kingdom, the eldest Pandava prince Yudhishthira having been induced to stake the fortunes of himself and his brethren on a game of dice, in which he was defeated; how the five Pandavas, with their common wife Draupadi (observe this curious and ugly feature of polyandry, which is quite opposed to standard Hindu morals, but is by no means unparalleled in early Indian literature) retired into exile for thirteen years, and then came back with a great army of allies, and after fierce and bloody battles with the Kauravas and their supporters in the plain of Kurukshetra at last gained the victory, slew the Kauravas, and established Yudhishthira as king in Hastinapura. Among the Pandavas the leading part is played by the eldest, Yudhishthira, and the third, Arjuna; of the others, Bhima, the second, is a Hercules notable only for his strength, courage, and fidelity, while the twins Nakula and Sahadeva are colourless figures. Krishna plays an important part in the story; for on the return of the Pāṇḍavas to fight the Kauravas he accompanies Arjuna as his charioteer, and on the eve of the first battle delivers to him a discourse on his religion, the Bhagavad-gita, or Lord's Song, which has become one of the most famous and powerful of all the sacred books of India. Now if the Mahabharata were as homogeneous even as the Iliad and Odyssey, which give us a fairly consistent and truthful picture of a single age, we should be in a very happy position. Unfortunately this is not the case. Our epic began as a Bharata, or Tale of the Bharata Clan, probably of very moderate bulk, not later than 600 b.c., and perhaps considerably earlier; and from that time onward it went on growing bigger and bigger for over a thousand years, as editors stuffed in new episodes and still longer discourses on nearly all the religious and philosophic doctrines admitted within the four walls of Hinduism, until it grew to its present immense bulk, which it claims to amount to 100,000 verses. Thus it pictures the thought not of one century but of more than ten, and we cannot feel sure of the date of any particular statement in it. Nevertheless we can distinguish in a general way between the old skeleton of the story, in which the theme is treated in simple epic fashion, society is far freer than in later days and no one objects to eating beef, from the additional matter, in which the tale is recast in a far more grandiose vein and is padded out with enormous quantities of moral, religious, and philosophic sermons. The religion too is different in the different parts. In the older portions the gods who are most popular are Indra, Agni, and Brahma—not the neuter abstract Brahma, but the masculine Brahma, the Demiurge, who corresponds more or less to Prajapati of the Brahmanas and is represented in classical art as a four-headed old man reciting the Vedas—and Krishna seems to figure only as a hero or at best as a demigod; but the later parts with fine impartiality claim the supremacy of heaven variously for Siva, Brahma, and Vishnu; and Vishnu, as we have seen, is sometimes identified with Krishna, notably in the chapters known as the Bhagavad-gita.

The gods have changed somewhat since earlier days. Indra has settled down in the constitutional monarchy of Paradise assigned to him by the Brahmanas; he now figures as the prototype of earthly kings, leading the armies of the gods to war against the demons when occasion requires, and passing the leisure of peace in the enjoyment of celestial dissipation. His morals have not improved: he is a debonair debauchee. Brahma the Creator, a more popular version of Prajapati, is still too impersonal to have much hold on the popular imagination; the same is the case with Agni the Fire-god. Plainly there was a vacancy for a supreme deity whose character was powerful enough to move men's souls, either through awe or love; and for this vacancy there were two strong candidates, Vishnu and Siva, who in course of time succeeded to the post and divided the supremacy between them.

Vishnu has altered immensely since last we met him. First, after an extraordinary change in his own character, he has been identified with Narayana, and then both of them have been equated with Krishna. The development is so portentous that it calls for a little study.

We have seen that in the Vedas Vishnu appears to be, and in the Brahmanas certainly is, the embodied Spirit of the Sacrifice, and that ritual mysticism has invented for him a supreme home in the highest heaven. But in the Epics he has developed into a radiant and gracious figure of ideal divinity, an almighty saviour with a long record of holy works for the salvation of mankind, a god who delights in moral goodness as well as in ritual propriety, and who from time to time incarnates himself in human or animal form so as to maintain the order of righteousness. Symbolism has further endowed him with a consort, the goddess Sri or Lakshmi, typifying fortune; sometimes also he is represented with another wife, the Earth-goddess. The divine hawk or kite Garuḍa, who seems to have been originally the same as the eagle who in the Rigvedic legend carried off the soma for Indra, has been pressed into his service; he now rides on Garuḍa, and bears his figure upon his banner. I have already suggested a possible explanation of this evolution (above, p. 41): owing to his close association with Indra, the most truly popular of Rigvedic deities, the laic imagination transfused some of the live blood of Indra into the veins of the priestly abstraction Vishnu. To the plain man Indra was very real; and as he frequently heard tales of Indra being aided in his exploits by Vishnu, he came to regard Vishnu as a very present helper in trouble. The friend of Indra became the friend of mankind. The post of Indra had already been fixed for him by the theologians; but the functions of Vishnu, outside the rituals, were still somewhat vaguely defined, and were capable of considerable expansion. Here was a great opportunity for those souls who were seeking for a supreme god of grace, and were not satisfied to find him in Siva; and they made full use of it, and wholly transformed the personality of Vishnu.

One of the stages in this transformation was the absorption of Narayana in Vishnu. Narayana was originally a god of a different kind. The earliest reference to him is in a Brahmana which calls him Purusha Narayana, which means that it regards him as being the same as the Universal Spirit which creates from itself the cosmos; it relates that Purusha Narayana pervaded the whole of nature (SB. XII. iii. 4, 1), and that he made himself omnipresent and supreme over all beings by performing a *pancha-ratra sattra*, or series of sacrifices lasting over five days (ib. XIII. vi. 1, 1). Somewhat later we find prayers addressed to Narayana, Vasudeva, and Vishnu as three phases of the same god (Taitt. Aran. X. i. 6). But was Narayana in origin merely a variety of the Vedic Purusha or our old acquaintance Prajapati? His name must give us pause. The most simple explanation of it is that it is a family name: as Karshnayana means a member of the Krishna-family and Ranayana a man belonging to the family of Rana, so Narayana would naturally denote a person of the family of Nara. But Nara itself signifies a *man*: is the etymology therefore reduced to absurdity? Not at all: Nara is also used as a proper name, as we shall see.[2] Probably the name really means what naturally it would seem to mean, «a man of the Nara family»; that Narayana was originally a divine or deified saint, a *rishi*, as the Hindus would call him; and that somehow he became identified with Vishnu and the Universal Spirit.

This theory really is not by any means as wild as at first sight it may seem to be. Divine saints are sometimes mentioned in the Rig-veda and Brahmanas as being the creators of the universe[3]; and they appear again and again in legend as equals of the gods, attaining divine powers by their mystic insight into the sacrificial lore. But there is more direct evidence than this.

In the Mahabharata there are incorporated two documents of first-rate importance for the doctrines of the churches that worshipped Vishnu. One of these is the Bhagavad-gita, or Lord's Song (VI. xxv.-xlii.); the other is the Narayaniya, or Account of Narayana (XII. cccxxxvi.-cccliii.). Their teachings are not the same in details, though on most main points they agree; for they belong to different sections of the one religious body. Leaving aside the Bhagavad-gita for the moment, we note that the Narayaniya relates a story that there were born four sons of Dharma, or Righteousness, viz. Nara, Narayana, Hari or Vishnu, and Krishna. In other places (I. ccxxx. 18, III. xii. 45, xlvii. 10, V. xlviii. 15, etc.) we are plainly told that Nara is a previous incarnation of Arjuna the Pandava prince, and Narayana is, of course, the supreme Deity, who in the time of Arjuna was born on earth as Krishna Vasudeva, and that in his earlier birth Nara and Narayana were both ascetic saints. This tradition is very important, for it enables us to see something of the early character of Narayana. He was an ancient saint of legend, who was connected with a hero Nara, just as Krishna was associated with Arjuna; and the atmosphere of saintliness clings to him obstinately. Tradition alleges that he was the *rishi*, or inspired seer, who composed the Purusha-sukta of the Rig-veda (X. 90), and represents him by choice as lying in a *yoga-nidra*, or mystic sleep, upon the body of the giant serpent Sesha in the midst of the Ocean of Milk. Thus the worship of Vishnu, like the worship of Siva, has owed much to the influence of live yogis idealised as divine saints; though it must be admitted that the yogis of the Vaishnava orders have usually been more agreeable and less ambiguous than those of the Saiva community.

We must briefly consider now the religious teachings of the Bhagavad-gita and the Narayaniya, and then turn to the inscriptions and contemporary literature to see whether we can find any sidelights in them. We begin with the Bhagavad-gita, or The Lord's Song.

The Bhagavad-gita purports to be a dialogue between the Pan ava prince Arjuna and Krishna, who was serving him as his charioteer, on the eve of the great battle. In order to invent a leading motive for his teaching, the poet represents Arjuna as suddenly stricken with overwhelming remorse at the prospect of the fratricidal strife which he is about to begin. "I will not fight," he cries in anguish. Then Krishna begins a long series of arguments to stimulate him for the coming battle. He points out, with quotations from the Upanishads, that killing men in battle does not destroy their souls; for the soul is indestructible, migrating from body to body according to its own deserts. The duty of the man born in the Warrior-caste is to fight; fighting is his caste-duty, his *dharma*, and as such it can entail upon him no guilt if it be performed in the right spirit. But how is this to be done? The answer is the leading motive of Krishna's teaching. For the maintenance of the world it is necessary that men should do the works of their respective castes, and these works do not operate as *karma* to the detriment of the future life of their souls if they perform them not from selfish motives but as offerings made in perfect unselfishness to the Lord. This is the doctrine of *Karma-yoga*, discipline of works, which is declared to lead the soul of the worshipper to salvation in the Lord as effectually as the ancient intellectualism preached in the Upanishads and the Samkhya philosophy. But there is also a third way to salvation, the way through loving devotion, or *bhakti*, which is as efficacious as either of the other two; the worshippers of Siva had already preached this for their own church in the Svetasvatara Upanishad. Besides treating without much consistency or method of many incidental questions of religious theory and practice, Krishna reveals himself for a few instants to Arjuna in his form as Viraj, the universal being in which all beings are comprehended and consumed. Finally Arjuna is comforted, and laying the burden of all his works upon Krishna, he prepares in quiet faith for the coming day of battle.

There are four main points to notice in this teaching. (1) The Supreme God, superior to Brahma, he who rules by grace and comprehends in his universal person the whole of existence, is Vishnu, or Hari, represented on earth for the time being by Krishna Vasudeva. The author makes no attempt to reconcile the fatalism implied in the old theory of *karma-samsara* with his new doctrine of special and general grace: he allows the two principles to stand side by side, and leaves for future generations of theologians the delicate task of harmonising them. (2) Three roads to salvation are recognised in principle, the intellectual gnosis of the old Upanishads and the Samkhya, the "way of works" or performance of necessary social duties in a spirit of perfect surrender to God, and the "way of devotion," continuous loving worship and contemplation of God. In practice the first method is ignored as being too severe for average men; the second and third are recommended, as being suitable for all classes. (3) The way of salvation is thus thrown open directly to men and women of all castes and conditions. The Bhagavad-gita fully approves of the orthodox division of society into castes; but by its doctrine that the performance of caste-duties in a spirit of sacrifice leads to salvation it makes caste an avenue to salvation, not a barrier. (4) The Bhagavad-gita has nothing to say for the animal-sacrifices of the Brahmans. It recognises only offerings of flowers, fruits, and the like. The doctrine of *ahimsa*, "thou shalt do no hurt," was making much headway at the time, and the wholesale animal-sacrifices of the Brahmans roused general disgust, of which the Buddhists and Jains took advantage for the propagation of their teachings.

I have previously spoken of the solitary passage in the Chhandogya Upanishad in which Krishna's name is mentioned, as receiving the teachings of Ghora Angirasa, and it will now be fitting to see how far these teachings are reflected in the Bhagavad-gita. Ghora compares the functions of life to the ceremonies of the *diksha* (see above, p.68): and this is at bottom the same idea as the doctrine of *karma-yoga* preached again and again in the Bhagavad-gita. "Whatever be thy work, thine eating, thy sacrifice, thy gift, thy mortification, make of it an offering to me," says Krishna (IX. 27); all life should be regarded as a sacrifice freely offered. Then Ghora continues: "In the hour of death one should take refuge in these three thoughts: 'Thou art the Indestructible, Thou art the Unfailing, Thou art instinct with Spirit.' On this there are these two verses of the Rig-veda:

Thus upward from the primal seedFrom out the darkness all aroundWe, looking on the higher light,Yea, looking on the higher heaven,Have come to Surya, god midst gods,To him that is the highest light, the highest light."

In the Bhagavad-gita (IV. 1 ff.) Krishna announces that he preached his doctrine to Vivasvan the Sun-god, who passed it on to his son the patriarch Manu; elsewhere in the Mahabharata (XII. cccv. 19) the Satvata teaching is said to have been announced by the Sun. Ghora in his list of moral virtues enumerates "mortification, charity, uprightness, harmlessness, truthfulness"; exactly the same attributes, with a few more, are said in the Bhagavad-gita to characterise the man who is born to the gods' estate (XVI. 1-3). Ghora's exhortation to think of the nature of the Supreme in the hour of death is balanced by Krishna's words: "He who at his last hour, when he casts off the body, goes hence remembering me, goes assuredly into my being" (VIII. 5; cf. 10). These parallels are indeed not very close; but collectively they are significant, and when we bear in mind that the author of the Bhagavad-gita is eager to associate his doctrine with those of the Upanishads, and thus to make it a new and catholic Upanishad for all classes, we are led to conclude that its fundamental ideas, sanctification of works (*karma-yoga*), worship of a Supreme God of Grace (*bhakti*) by all classes, and rejection of animal sacrifices (*ahimsa*) arose among the orthodox Kshatriyas, who found means to persuade their Brahmanic preceptors to bring it into connection with their Upanishads and embellish it with appropriate texts from those sources. Very likely Krishna Vasudeva, if not the first inventor of these doctrines, was their most vigorous propagator.

Now what are the teachings of the Narayaniya? It appears to contain two accounts. In the first we have the story of king Vasu Uparichara, who is said to have worshipped the Supreme God Hari (Vishnu) in devotion without any animal-sacrifices, in accordance with doctrines ascribed to the Aranyakas, i.e. the later sections of the Brahmanas, including the older Upanishads. This fully agrees with the standpoint of the Bhagavad-gita. The second account gives the story of a visit paid by the divine saint Narada to a mysterious "White Island," Sveta-dvipa, inhabited by holy worshippers of God who are, strangely enough, described as having heads shaped like umbrellas and feet like lotus-leaves and as making a sound like that of thunder-clouds[4]; they are radiant like the moon, have no physical senses, eat nothing, and concentrate their whole soul on rapturous adoration of the spirit of God, which shines there in dazzling brightness to the eye of perfect faith. Narayana there reveals himself to Narada, and sets forth to him the doctrine of Vasudeva. According to this, Narayana has four forms, called *murtis* or *vyuhas*. The first of these is Vasudeva, who is the highest soul and creator and inwardly controls all individual souls. From him arose Samkarshana, who corresponds to the individual soul; from Samkarshana issued Pradyumna, to whom corresponds the organ of mind, and from Pradyumna came forth Aniruddha, representing the element of self-consciousness. Observe in passing that these are all names of heroes of legend: Samkarshana is Vasudeva's brother Bala-rama, Pradyumna was the son and Aniruddha the grandson of Vasudeva. Narayana then goes on to speak of the creation of all things from himself and their dissolution into himself, and of his incarnations in the form of the Boar who lifted up on his tusk the earth when submerged under the ocean, Narasimha the Man-lion who destroyed the tyrant Hiranya-kasipu, the Dwarf who overthrew Bali, Rama Bhargava who destroyed the Kshatriyas, Rama Dasarathi, of whom we shall have something to say later. Krishna Vasudeva the slayer of Kamsa of Mathura, the Tortoise, the Fish, and Kalki. Then follow some further details, among them a statement that this doctrine was revealed to Arjuna at the beginning of the Great War—a clear reference to the Bhagavad-gita—that at the beginning of every age it was promulgated by Narayana, that it requires activity in pious works, that at the commencement of the present age it passed from him to Brahma, from him to Vivasvan the Sun-god, from him to the patriarch Manu, etc., that it does not allow the sacrifice of animals, and that for salvation the co-operative grace of Narayana is necessary. Most of this doctrine is already in the Bhagavad-gita; what is not found in the latter is the account of the mysterious White Island, the theory of *vyuhas* or emanations, which represents Vasudeva as issuing from Narayana and so forth, and the details of Narayana's incarnations. It is therefore a distinct textbook of the Satvata or Pancharatra church, not much later than the Bhagavad-gita. According to it, the Supreme Being is Narayana, the Almighty God who reveals himself as highest teacher and saintly sage, whose legendary performance of a five-days' sacrifice (above, p. 76) has gained for his doctrine the title of Pancharatra. Next in order of divinity is Krishna Vasudeva, whose tribal name of Satvata has furnished the other name of this church; then follow in due order Samkarshana, Pradyumna, and Aniruddha, all of his family; and with Vasudeva is closely associated the epic hero Arjuna, a prototype for this mortal pair being discovered in the legendary Nara and Narayana.

Comparing then the Bhagavad-gita with the Narayaniya, we see that in all essentials they agree, but in two points they differ. Both preach a doctrine of activity in pious works, *pravritti*, in conscious opposition to the inactivity of the Aupanishadas and Samkhyas; but the Narayaniya does not dwell much on this topic, and limits activity to strictly religious duties, while the Bhagavad-gita develops the idea so as to include everything, thus sketching out a bold system for the sanctification of all sides of life, which enables it to open the door of salvation directly to all classes of mankind. Secondly, the Bhagavad-gita says nothing about the theory of emanations or *vyuhas* in connection with Vasudeva; probably its author knew the legends of Samkarshana, Pradyumna, and Aniruddha, but he apparently did not know or at least did not accept the view that these persons were related as successive emanations from Vasudeva. We must therefore look round for sidelights which may clear up the obscurities in the history of this church.

Our first sidelight glimmers in the famous grammar of Panini, who probably lived in the fifth century B.C., or perhaps early in the fourth century. Panini informs us (IV. iii. 98) that from the names of Vasudeva and Arjuna the derivative nouns *Vasudevaka* and *Arjunaka* are formed to denote persons who worship respectively Vasudeva and Arjuna. Plainly then in the fifth century Krishna Vasudeva and Arjuna were worshipped by some, probably in the same connection as is shown in the Mahabharata. Perhaps Vasudeva had not yet been raised to the rank of the Almighty; it is more likely that he was still a deified hero and teacher, and Arjuna his noblest disciple. But both of them were receiving divine honours; they had been men, and were now gods, with bands of adorers.

Our next evidence is an inscription found not long ago on the base of a stone column at Besnagar near Bhilsa, in the south of Gwalior State,[5] and must have been engraved soon after 200 B.C. It reads as follows: «This Garuda-column of Vasudeva the god of gods was erected here by Heliodorus, a worshipper of the Lord [*bhagavata*], the son of Diya [Greek *Dion*] and an inhabitant of Taxila, who came as ambassador of the Greeks from the Great King Amtalikita [Greek *Antialcidas*] to King Kasiputra Bhagabhadra the Saviour, who was flourishing in the fourteenth year of his reign"; and below this are two lines in some kind of verse, which announce that "three immortal steps ... when practised lead to heaven—self-control, charity, and diligence." Here, then, in the centre of a thriving kingdom probably forming part of the Sunga empire, Vasudeva is worshipped not as a minor hero or teacher, but as the god of gods, *deva-deva*; and he is worshipped by the Greek Heliodorus, visiting the place as an ambassador from Antialcidas, a Hellenic king of the lineage of Eucratides, who was reigning in the North-West of India. Doubtless the act of Heliodorus was a diplomatic courtesy, in order to please King Kasiputra Bhagabhadra. But observe the nature of his act. He caused to be erected a Garu a-column, that is, a pillar engraved with the figure of Garu a, the sacred bird of Vishnu; and he added a verse about "three immortal steps" (*trini amutapadani*), as leading to heaven, which sounds suspiciously like an attempt to moralise the old mythical feature of the three Steps of Vishnu. Plainly Vasudeva had now risen in this part of the country from being the teacher of a church of Vishnu-Narayana to the rank of its chief god, with which he had become fully identified.

Another inscription, a few years later in date, has been found in Besnagar. It is a mere fragment, but it supplements the other;

for it states that a certain *bhagavata*, or "worshipper of the Lord," named Gotama-puta (Gautama-putra in Sanskrit) erected a Garuda-column for the Lord's temple in the twelfth year from the coronation of King Bhagavata. This king is perhaps the same as the person of that name who appears in some genealogical lists as the last but one of the Sunga Kings.[6]

Next in date is an inscription on a stone slab found at Ghasundi, about four miles north-east of Nagari, in Udaipur State. It was engraved about 150 B.C., and records that a certain *bhagavata*, or "worshipper of the Lord," named Gajayana, son of Parasari, caused to be erected in the Narayana-vata, or park of Narayana, a stone chapel for the worship of the Lords Samkarshana and Vasudeva.[7] Here their worship is associated with that of Narayana.

Passing over an inscription at Mathura which records the building of a part of a sanctuary to the Lord Vasudeva about 15 B.C. by the great Satrap Sodasa,[8] we note that the grammarian Patanjali, who wrote his commentary the Mahabhashya upon Panini's grammar about 150 B.C., has something to say about Krishna Vasudeva, whom he recognises as a divine being (on IV. iii. 98). He quotes some verses referring to him. The first (on II. ii. 23) is to the following effect: "May the might of Krishna accompanied by Samkarshana increase!" Another (on VI. iii. 6) speaks of "Janardana with himself as fourth," that is to say, Krishna with three companions: the three may be Samkarshana, Pradyumna, and Aniruddha, or they may not. Another verse (on II. ii. 34) speaks of musical instruments being played at meetings in the temples of Rama and Kesava. Rama is Bala-rama or Bala-bhadra, who is the same as Samkarshana, and Kesava is a title of Krishna, which was applied also to Vishnu or Narayana according to the Bodhayana-dharma-sutra, which may be assigned to the second century B.C. The Ovavai, or Aupapatika-sutra, a Jain scripture which may perhaps belong to the same period, mentions (§ 76) *Kanha-parivvaya*, wandering friars who worshipped Krishna. Thus literature as well as inscriptions shows that Krishna Vasudeva and his brother Samkarshana were in many places worshipped as saints of a church of Vishnu-Narayana about 150 B.C., and that in some parts Vasudeva was recognised as the Almighty himself about 200 B.C.

In another passage (on III. i, 26) Patanjali describes dramatic and mimetic performances representing the killing of Kamsa by Vasudeva. Altogether his references show that the legend and worship of Vasudeva bulked largely in the popular mind at this time in India north of the Vindhya mountains. Vasudeva was adored as the great teacher and hero-king, in whom the gods Vishnu and Narayana were incarnated; and he was associated with two great cycles of legend, the one that related his birth at Mathura, his victory over the tyrant Kamsa, his establishment of the colony at Dvaraka, and his adventures until his death and translation to heaven, and the other telling of his share in the Great War as ally of the five Pandava brethren. Both cycles represented him as supported by princely heroes. The Mathura-Dvaraka legend gave him his brother Bala-bhadra or Samkarshana, his son Pradyumna, and his grandson Aniruddha, whom theologians about the beginning of the Christian era fitted into their philosophical schemes by representing them as successive emanations from him; and the Mahabharata furnished him with the Pandavas, whose heroic tale soon created for them a worship everywhere. As we have seen, there were adorers of Arjuna already in the fifth century B.C.; and in the first century B.C. there seems to be evidence for a worship of all the five together with Vasudeva, for an inscription has been found at Mora which apparently mentions a son of the great Satrap Rajuvula, probably the well-known Satrap Sodasa, and an image of the "Lord Vrishni," probably Vasudeva, and of the "Five Warriors."[9] Already the poets of the Mahabharata have taken the first step towards the deification of the Pandavas by finding divine fathers for each of them, making Yudhishthira the son of Dharma or Yama, the god of the nether world, Arjuna son of Indra, Bhima son of Vayu the Wind-god, and Nakula and Sahadeva offspring of the Asvins. Hundreds of caverns throughout India are declared by popular legend to have been their dwellings during their wanderings; and a noble monument to their memory has been raised by one of the great Pallava kings of Conjevaram who in the seventh century A.D. carved out of the solid rock on the seashore at Mamallapuram the fine chapels that bear their names. Doubtless all these heroes from both cycles were once worshipped in the usual manner, with offerings of food, incense, lights, flowers, etc., and singing of hymns on their exploits—chiefly in connection with Vasudeva; but all this worship is now utterly forgotten, except where echoes of it linger in popular legend.

Our survey of the religion of Vasudeva has brought us down to a date which cannot indeed be exactly fixed, but which may be placed approximately in the second century of our era. This religion, as we have seen, arose and grew great in the fertile soil of the spiritual needs and experiences of India. It began by moulding a personal God out of ancient figures of myth and legend, and it surrounded him with a hierarchy of godly heroes. Though its doctrines were often philosophically incongruous and incoherent, its foundation was a true religious feeling; it gave scope to the mystic raptures of the ascetic and the simple righteousness of the laic; and it claimed for its heroes, Vasudeva and his kindred and his friends the Pandava brethren, a grave and dignified hero-worship. In short, it is a serious Indian religion with an epic setting.

And now suddenly and most unexpectedly an utterly new spirit begins to breathe in it. To the old teachings and legends are added new ones of a wholly different cast. The old epic spirit of grave and manly chivalry and godly wisdom is overshadowed by a new passion—adoration of tender babyhood and wanton childhood, amorous ecstasies, a hectic fire of erotic romance.

Of this new spirit there is no trace in the epic, except in one or two late interpolations. But the Hari-vamsa, which was added as an appendix to the Mahabharata not very long before the fourth century A.D., is already instinct with it. It adds to the epic story of Krishna a fluent verse account of his miraculous preservation from Kamsa at his birth, his childhood among the herdsmen and herdswomen of Vraja (the Doab near Mathura) with its marvellous freaks and wonderful exploits, his amorous sports with the herdswomen, in fact all the sensuous emotionalism on which the later church of Krishna has ever since battened. About the same time appeared the Vishnu-purana, which includes most of the same matter as the Hari-vamsa; and some centuries later, probably about the tenth century, there was written a still more remarkable book, the Bhagavata-purana, of which a great part is taken up with the romance of Krishna's babyhood and childhood, and especially his amorous sports. In the Bhagavata the later worship of Krishna found its classic expression. In the Hari-vamsa and Vishnu-purana religious emotion is still held under a certain restraint; but in the Bhagavata it has broken loose and runs riot. It is a romance of ecstatic love for Krishna, who is no longer, as in the Vishnu-purana, the incarnation of a portion of the Supreme Vishnu, but very God become man, wholly and utterly divine in his humanity. It dwells in a rapture of tenderness upon the God-babe, and upon the wanton play of the lovely child who is delightful in his naughtiness and marvellous in his occasional displays of superhuman power; it figures him as an ideal of boyish beauty, decked with jewels and crested with peacock's feathers, wandering through the flowering forests of Vraja, dancing and playing on his flute melodies that fill the souls of all that hear them with an irresistible passion of love and delight; it revels in tales of how the precocious boy made wanton sport with the herdswomen of Vraja, and how the magic of his fluting drew them to the dance in which they were united to him in a rapture of love. The book thrills with amorous, sensuous ecstasy; the thought of Krishna stirs the worshipper to a passion of love in which tears gush forth in the midst of laughter, the speech halts, and often the senses fail and leave him in long trances. Erotic emotionalism can go no further.

Where did this new spirit come from? Some have laboured to prove that it had its source in Christianity; others have argued that it was Christianity that was the debtor to India in this respect. Both theories are in the main impossible. This cult of the child Krishna arose in India, and, with the possible exception of a few obscure tales, it never spread outside the circle of Indian religion. But how and where did it arise? That is a question hard to answer; there is no direct evidence, and we can only balance probabilities. Now what are the probabilities?

The worship of Krishna as a babe, a boy, and a young man among the herdsfolk of Vraja seems to have no relation with the older form of the religion as set forth in the epic textbooks. It is a new element, imported from without. The most natural conclusion then is that it came from the people who are described in it, some tribe that pastured their herds in the woodlands near Mathura. Perhaps these herdsfolk were Abhiras, ancestors of the modern Ahir tribes. If so, it would be natural that their cult should attract attention; for sometimes Abhiras counted for something in society, and we even find a short-lived dynasty of Abhira kings reigning in Nasik in the third century A.D.[10] Be this as it may, it seems very likely that some pastoral tribe had a cult of a divine child blue or black of hue, and perhaps actually called by them Krishna or Kanha, "Black-man" (observe that henceforth Krishna is regularly represented with a blue skin), a cult in which gross rustic fantasy had free play; that it came in some circles to be linked on to the epic cycle of Krishna Vasudeva; and that some Bhagavatas, seeing in it latent possibilities, gave it polished literary expression and thereby established it as a part of the Vasudeva legend. It quickly seized upon the popular imagination and spread like wild-fire over India. For it satisfied many needs. The tenderness of the father and still more of the mother for the little babe, their delight in the sports of childhood, the amorist's pleasure in erotic adventure, and, not by any means least, the joy in the romantic scenery of the haunted woodlands—all these instincts found full play in it, and were sanctified by religion.

II. Rama

Rama is the hero of the Ramayana, the great epic ascribed to Valmiki, a poet who in course of time has passed from the realm of history into that of myth, like many other Hindus. The poem, as it has come down to us, contains seven books, which relate the following tale. Dasa-ratha, King of Ayodhya (now Ajodhya, near Faizabad), of the dynasty which claimed descent from the Sun-god, had no son, and therefore held the great *Asva-medha*, or horse-sacrifice, as a result of which he obtained four sons, Rama by his queen Kausalya, Bharata by Kaikeyi, and Lakshmana and

Satrughna by Sumitra. Rama, the eldest, was also pre-eminent for strength, bravery, and noble qualities of soul. Visiting in his early youth the court of Janaka, king of Videha, Rama was able to shoot an arrow from Janaka's bow, which no other man could bend, and as a reward he received as wife the princess Sita, whom Janaka had found in a furrow of his fields and brought up as his own daughter. So far the first book, or Bala-kanda. The second book, or Ayodhya-kanda, relates how Queen Kaikeyi induced Dasa-ratha, sorely against his will, to banish Rama to the forests in order that her son Bharata might succeed to the throne; and the Aranya-kanda then describes how Rama, accompanied by his wife Sita and his faithful brother Lakshmana, dwelt in the forest for a time, until the demon King Ravana of Lanka, by means of a trick, carried off Sita to his city. The Kishkindha-kanda tells of Rama's pursuit of Ravana and his coming to Kishkindha, the city of Sugriva, the king of the apes, who joined him as an ally in his expedition; and the Sundara-kanda describes the march of their armies to Lanka, which is identified with Ceylon, and their crossing over the straits. Then comes the Yuddha-kanda, which narrates the war with Ravana, his death in battle, the restoration of Sita, the return of Rama and Sita to Ayodhya, and the crowning of Rama in place of Dasa-ratha, who had died of grief during his exile. Finally comes the Uttara-kanda, which relates that Rama, hearing some of the people of Ayodhya spitefully casting aspersions on the virtue of Sita during her imprisonment in the palace of Ravana, gave way to foolish jealousy and banished her to the hermitage of Valmiki, where she gave birth to twin sons, Kusa and Lava; when these boys had grown up, Valmiki taught them the Ramayana and sent them to sing it at the court of Rama, who on hearing it sent for Sita, who came to him accompanied by Valmiki, who assured him of her purity; and then Sita swore to it on oath, calling upon her mother the Earth-goddess to bear witness; and the Earth-goddess received her back into her bosom, leaving Rama bereaved, until after many days he was translated to heaven.

Such is the tale of Rama as told in the Valmiki-ramayana—a clean, wholesome story of chivalry, love, and adventure. But clearly the Valmiki-ramayana is not the work of a single hand. We can trace in it at least two strata. Books II.-VI. contain the older stratum; the rest is the addition of a later poet or series of poets, who have also inserted some padding into the earlier books. This older stratum, the nucleus of the epic, gives us a picture of heroic society in India at a very early date, probably not very long after the age of the Upanishads; perhaps we shall not be far wrong if we say it was composed some time before the fourth century B.C. In it Rama is simply a hero, miraculous in strength and goodness, but nevertheless wholly human; but in the later stratum—Books I. and VII. and the occasional insertions in the other books—conditions are changed, and Rama appears as a god on earth, a partial incarnation of Vishnu, exactly as in the Bhagavad-gita and other later parts of the Mahabharata the hero Krishna has become an incarnation of Vishnu also. The parallel may even be traced further. Krishna stands to Arjuna in very much the same relation as Rama to his brother Lakshmana—a greater and a lesser hero, growing into an incarnate god and his chief follower. This is thoroughly in harmony with Hindu ideas, which regularly conceive the teacher as accompanied by his disciple and abhor the notion of a voice crying in the wilderness; indeed we may almost venture to suspect that this symmetry in the epics is not altogether uninfluenced by this ideal. This, however, is a detail: the main point to observe is that Rama was originally a local hero of the Solar dynasty, a legendary king of Ayodhya, and as the Puranas give him a full pedigree, there is no good reason to doubt that he really existed "once upon a time." But the story with which he is associated in the Ramayana is puzzling. Is it a pure romance? Or is it a glorified version of some real adventures? Or can it be an old tale, perhaps dating from the early dawn of human history, readapted and fitted on to the person of an historical Rama? The first of these hypotheses seems unlikely, though by no means impossible. The second suggestion has found much favour. Many have believed that the story of the expedition of Rama and his army of apes to Lanka represents a movement of the Aryan invaders from the North towards the South; and this is supported to some extent by Indian tradition, which has located most of the places mentioned in the Ramayana, and in particular has identified Lanka with Ceylon. In support of this one may point to the Iliad of Homer, which has a somewhat similar theme, the rape and recovery of Helen by the armies of the Achæans, the basis of which is the historical fact of an expedition against Troy and the destruction of that city. But there are serious difficulties in the way of accepting this analogy, the most serious of all being the indubitable fact that there is not a tittle of evidence to show that such an expedition was ever made by the Aryans. True, there were waves of emigration from Aryan centres southward in early times; but those that travelled as far as Ceylon went by sea, either from the coasts of Bengal or Orissa or Bombay. Besides, the expedition of Rama is obviously fabulous, for his army was composed not of Aryans but of apes. All things considered, there seems to be most plausibility in the third hypothesis[11]. Certainly Rama was a local hero of Ayodhya, and probably he was once a real king; so it is likely enough that an old saga (or sagas) attached itself early to his memory. And as his fame spread abroad, principally on the wings of Valmiki's poem, the honours of semi-divinity began to be paid to him in many places beyond his native land, and about the beginning of our era he was recognised as an incarnation of Vishnu sent to establish a reign of righteousness in the world. In Southern India this cult of Rama, like that of Krishna, has for the most part remained subordinate to the worship of Vishnu, though the Vaishnava church there has from early times recognised the divinity of both of them as embodiments of the Almighty. But its great home is the North, where millions worship Rama with passionate and all-absorbing love.

III. Some Later Preachers

With all its attractions and success, the new Krishnaism did not everywhere overgrow the older stock upon which it had been engrafted. There were many places in which the early worship of Vishnu and Vasudeva remained almost unchanged. The new legends of Krishna's childhood might indeed be accepted in these centres of conservatism, but they made little difference in the spirit and form of the worship, which continued to follow the ancient order. In some of them the Bhagavad-gita, Narayaniya, and other epic doctrinals still remained the standard texts, which theologians connected with the ancient Upanishads and the Brahma-sutra summarising the latter; in other centres there arose, beginning perhaps about the seventh century A.D., a series of Samhitas, or manuals of doctrine and practice for the Pancharatra[12] sect, which, though in essentials agreeing with the Narayaniya, taught a different theory of cosmogony and introduced the worship of the goddess Sri or Lakshmi, the consort of Vishnu, as the agency or energy through which the Supreme Being becomes active in finite existence; and in yet other places other texts were followed, such as those of the Vaikhanasa school. This worship of Vishnu-Vasudeva on the ancient lines was peculiarly vigorous among the representatives of Aryan culture in the South, who had introduced the cults of Vishnu and Siva with the rest of the Aryan pantheon into the midst of Dravidian animism. Hinduism, transplanted into the Dravidian area, has there remained more conservative than anywhere else, and has clung firmly to its ancient traditions. There is nothing of Dravidian origin in the South Indian worship of Vishnu and Siva; they are entirely Aryan importations. But they have become thoroughly assimilated in their southern home, and each of them has produced a huge mass of fine devotional literature in the vernaculars. In the Tamil country the church of Vishnu boasts of the Nal-ayira-prabandham, a collection of Tamil psalms numbering about 4,000 stanzas composed by twelve poets called Alvars, which were collected about 1000 A.D.; and the worship of 'Siva is equally well expressed in the Tiru-murai, compiled about the twelfth century, of which one section, the Devaram, was put together about the same time as the Nal-ayira-prabandham. Both the Tiru-murai and the Nal-ayira-prabandham breathe the same spirit of ecstatic devotion as the Bhagavata-purana; they are the utterances of wandering votaries who travelled from temple to temple and poured forth the passionate raptures of their souls in lyrical praise of their deities. Through these three main channels the stream of devotion spread far and wide through the land. Like most currents of what we call "revivalism," it usually had an erotic side; and the larger temples frequently have attached to them female staffs of attendant votaries and *corps de ballet* of very easy virtue. But this aspect was far more marked in neo-Krishnaism, which often tends to intense pruriency, than in the other two cults. The Alvars pay little regard to the legends of Krishna, and concentrate their energies upon the worship of Vishnu as he is represented in the great temples of Srirangam, Conjevaram, Tirupati, and similar sanctuaries.

About the beginning of the ninth century the peaceful course of Vaishnava religion was rudely disturbed by the preaching of Samkara Acharya. Samkara, one of the greatest intellects that India has ever produced, was a Brahman of Malabar, and was born about the year 788. Taking his stand upon the Upanishads, Brahma-sutra, and Bhagavad-gita, upon which he wrote commentaries, he interpreted them as teaching the doctrine of Advaita, thorough monistic idealism, teaching that the universal Soul, Brahma, is absolutely identical with the individual Soul, the *atma* or Self, that all being is only one, that salvation consists in the identification of these two, and is attained by knowledge, the intuition of their identity, and that the phenomenal universe or manifold of experience is simply an illusion (*maya*) conjured up in Brahma by his congenital nature, but really alien to him—in fact, a kind of disease in Brahma. This was not new: it had been taught by some ancient schools of Aupanishadas, and was very like the doctrine of some of the Buddhist idealists; but the vigour and skill with which Samkara propagated his doctrines threatened ruin to orthodox Vaishnava theologians, and roused them to counter-campaigns. Among the Vaishnava Brahmans of the South who won laurels in this field was Yamunacharya, who lived about 1050, and was the grandson of Natha Muni, who collected the hymns of the Alvars in the Nal-ayira-prabandham and founded the great school of Vaishnava theology at Srirangam. In opposition to Samkara's monism, Yamunacharya propounded the doctrine of his school, the so-called Visishṭadvaita, which was preached with still greater skill and success by his famous successor Ramanuja, who died in 1137. Ramanuja's greatest works are his commentaries on the Brahma-sutra and Bhagavad-gita. In them he expounds with great ability the principles of his school, namely, that God, sentient beings or souls, and insentient matter form three essentially distinct classes of being; that God, who is the same as Brahma, Vishnu, Narayana, or Krishna, is omnipotent, omnipresent, and possessed of all good qualities; that matter forms the body of souls, and souls form the body of God; that the soul attains salvation as a result of devout and loving meditation upon God, worship of him, and study of the scriptures; and that salvation consists in eternal union of the soul with God, but not in identity with him, as Samkara taught. The scriptures on which Ramanuja took his stand were mainly the Upanishads, Brahma-sutra, and Bhagavad-gita; but he also acknowledged as authoritative the Pancharatra Samhitas, in spite of their divergences in details of doctrine, and it is from them that his church has derived the worship of Sri or Lakshmi as consort of Vishnu, which is a very marked feature of their community and has gained for them the title of Sri-vaishnavas. But Ramanuja was much more than a scholar and a writer of books; he was also a man of action, a "practical mystic." Like Samkara, he organised a body of *sannyasis* or ascetic votaries, into which, however, he admitted only Brahmans, whereas Samkara opened some of the sections of his devotees to non-Brahmans; but on the other hand he was far more liberal than Samkara in the choice of his congregations, for he endeavoured to bring men of the lowest castes, Sudras and even Pariahs, within the influence of his church, though he kept up the social barrier between them and the higher castes, and he firmly upheld the principle of the Bhagavad-gita that it is by the performance of religious and social duties of caste, and not by knowledge alone, that salvation is most surely to be won. He established schools and monasteries, reorganised the worship of the temples, usually in accordance with the Pancharatra rules, and thus placed his church in a position of such strength in Southern India that its only serious rival is the church of Siva.

Nimbarka, who probably flourished about the first half of the twelfth century, preached for the cult of Krishna a doctrine combining monism with dualism, which is followed by a small sect in Northern India. Ananda-tirtha or Madhva, in the first three quarters of the thirteenth century, propounded for the same church a theory of thorough dualism, which has found many admirers, chiefly in the Dekkan. Vallabhacharya, born in 1479, founded a school of Krishna-worshippers which claims a "pure monism" without the aid of the theory of *maya*, or illusion, which is a characteristic of Samkara's monism. This community has become very influential, chiefly in Bombay Presidency; but in recent times it has been under a cloud owing to the scandals arising from a tendency to practise immoral orgies and from the claims of its priesthood, as representing the god, to enjoy the persons and property of their congregations.

Besides these and other schools which were founded on a basis of Sanskrit scholastic philosophy, there have been many popular religious movements, which from the first appealed directly to the heart of the people in their own tongues.

The first place in which we see this current in movement is the Maratha country. Here, about 1290, Jnanesvara or Jnanadeva, popularly known as Jnanoba, composed his Jnanesvari, a paraphrase of the Bhagavad-gita in about 10,000 Marathi verses, as well as a number of hymns to Krishna and a poem on the worship of Siva. To the same period belonged Namadeva, who was born at Pandharpur, according to some in 1270 and according to others about a century later. Then came Ekanatha, who is said to have died in 1608, and composed some hymns and Marathi verse-translations from the Bhagavata. The greatest of all was Tukaram, who was born about 1608.[13] In the verses of these poets the worship of Krishna is raised to a level of high spirituality. Ramananda, who apparently lived between 1400 and 1470 and was somehow connected with the school of Ramanuja, preached salvation through Rama to all castes and classes of Northern India, with immense and enduring success. To his spiritual lineage belongs Tulsi Das (1532-1623), whose Rama-charita-manasa, a poem in Eastern Hindi on the story of Valmiki's Ramayana, has become the Bible of the North. The same influences are visible in the poems of Kabir, a Moslem by birth, who combined Hindu and Muhammadan doctrines into an eclectic monotheism, and is worshipped as an incarnation of God by his sect. He died in 1518. A kindred spirit was Nanak, the founder of the Sikh church (1469-1538).[14]

By the side of these upward movements there have been many which have remained on the older level of the Bhagavata. The most important is that of Visvambhara Misra, who is better known by his titles of Chaitanya and Gauranga (1485-1533); he carried on a "revival" of volcanic intensity in Bengal and Orissa, and the church founded by him is still powerful, and worships him as an incarnation of Krishna.

IV. Brahma and the Trimurti

Brahma, the Creator, a masculine noun, must be carefully distinguished from the neuter *Brahma*, the abstract First Being. The latter comes first in the scale of existence, while the former appears at some distance further on as the creator of the material world (see above, p. 60 f.). In modern days Brahma has been completely eclipsed by Vishnu and Siva and even by some minor deities, and has now only four temples dedicated to his exclusive worship.[15] But there was a time when he was a great god. In the older parts of the Mahabharata and Ramayana he figures as one of the greater deities, perhaps the greatest. But in the later portions of the epic he has shrunk into comparative insignificance as compared to Vishnu and Siva, and especially to Vishnu. This change faithfully reflects historical facts. During the last four or five centuries of the millennium which ended with the Christian era the orthodox Vedic religion of the Brahmans had steadily lost ground, and the sects worshipping Vishnu and Siva had correspondingly grown in power and finally had come to be recognised as themselves orthodox. Brahma, as his name implies, is the ideal Brahman sage, and typifies Vedic orthodoxy. He is represented as everlastingly chanting the four Vedas from his four mouths (for he has four heads), and he bears the water-pot and rosary of eleocarpus berries, the symbols of the Brahman ascetic. But Vedic orthodoxy had to make way for more fascinating cults, and the Vedic Brahman typified in the god Brahma sank into comparative unimportance beside the sectarian ascetics. Still the old god, though shorn of much of his glory, was by no means driven from the field. The new churches looked with reverence upon his Vedas, and often claimed them as divine authority for their doctrines; and though each of them asserted that its particular god, Siva or Vishnu, was the Supreme Being, and ultimately the only being, both of them allowed Brahma to retain his old office of creator, it being of course understood that he held it as a subordinate of the Supreme, Siva or Vishnu as the case might be. Meanwhile, at any rate between the third and the sixth centuries, there existed a small fraternity who regarded Brahma as the Supreme, and therefore as identical with the abstract Brahma; but although they have left a record of their doctrines in the Markandeya-purana and the Padma-purana, they have had little influence on Indian religion in general.

A love of system—unfortunately not always effectual—is a notable feature of the Hindu mind in dealing with most subjects, from grammar to *Ars Amoris*; and this instinct inspired some unknown theologian with the idea of harmonising the three gods into a unity by representing in one compound form or *Trimurti* Brahma as creator, Vishnu as the sustaining power in the universe, and Siva as the force of dissolution which periodically brings the cosmos to an end and necessitates in due course new cycles of being.[16] This ingenious plan has the advantage that it is without prejudice to the religion of any of the gods concerned, for all the three members of this trinity are subordinate to the Supreme Being, or Param Brahma, whom the Vaishnavas identify with Vishnu in his highest phase, Para-Vasudeva, and distinguish from his lower phase, the Vishnu of this compound, while the Saivas draw a corresponding distinction between Parama-Siva, the god in his transcendent nature, and the Siva who figures in the Trimurti. So the most orthodox Vaishnava and the most bigoted Saiva can adore this three-headed image of the Trimurti side by side with easy consciences.

This idea of the three gods in one, though it is embodied in some important works of sculpture such as the famous Trimurti in the Caves of Elephanta, has not had much practical effect upon Hindu religion. But it has given birth to at any rate one interesting little sect, the worshippers of Dattatreya, who are to be found mainly in the Maratha country. The legend of the saint Dattatreya, which is already found in the Mahabharata and Puranas and is repeated with some modifications and amplifications in modern works of the sect,[17] relates that when the holy Rishi Atri subjected himself to terrific austerities in order to obtain worthy progeny, the gods Brahma, Vishnu, and Siva visited him and promised him the desired boon; accordingly his wife Anasuya gave birth to three sons, of whom the first was the Moon, an incarnation of Brahma, the second Dattatreya, an incarnation of Vishnu, and the third the holy but irascible saint Durvasas, representing Siva. Dattatreya dwelt in a hermitage in the Dekkan: he indulged in marriage and wine-drinking, which however were not detrimental to his miraculous sanctity and wisdom, and he became famous as a benefactor to humanity. He is said to have lived in the time of Kartavirya Arjuna, the Haihaya king, and to have counselled the latter to remain on his throne when he wished to resign it. In older works of plastic art he is sometimes represented by the simple expedient of placing the three gods side by side, sometimes by figuring him as Vishnu in the guise of a Yogi with some of the attributes of the other two; but in modern times he usually appears as a single figure with three heads, one for each of the great gods, and four or six arms bearing their several attributes (usually the rosary and water-pot of Brahma, the conch and discus of Vishnu, and the trident and drum of Siva), while he is accompanied by four dogs of different colours, supposed to represent the four Vedas, and a bull.[18] Observe that in all these types Dattatreya is conceived as an embodiment of the three gods, which is comparatively a later idea, for in the oldest version of the legend he was simply an incarnation of Vishnu; but as Vishnu was regarded not only as a member of the Trinity but also the Supreme Being over and above it, Dattatreya as his representative has come to include in his personality the nature of all the trio. There is, moreover, something curious in his character. His love of wine and woman is a singular trait, and is quite incompatible with the nature of an ideal saint. It smells of reality, and strongly suggests that he was not a figment of the religious imagination but an actual man; and this is supported by the tradition of his association with Kartavirya Arjuna, who, in spite of all the mythical tales that are related of him, really seems to have been a king of flesh and blood.

Thus we may venture to see in him yet another example of the metamorphosis so common in India from a saint to an incarnation of the god worshipped by him.

V. Two Modern Instances

In Northern India, and especially in Bengal, you will often find Hindus worshipping a god whom they call Satya-narayana and believe to be an embodiment of Vishnu himself. The observance of this ritual is believed to bring wealth and all kinds of good fortune; a Sanskrit sacred legend in illustration of this belief has been created, and you may buy badly lithographed copies of it in most of the bazaars if you like, besides which you will find elegant accounts of the god's career on earth written by quite a number of distinguished Bengali poets of the last three centuries. But curiously enough this "god," though quite real, was not a Hindu at all; he was a Bengali Moslem, a fakir, and the Muhammadans of Bengal, among whom he is known as Satya Pir, have their own versions of his career, which seem to be much nearer the truth than those of the Hindus. In their stories he figures simply as a saint, who busied himself in performing miracles for the benefit of pious Moslems in distress; and as one legend says that he was the son of a daughter of [H.]usain Shah, the Emperor of Gaur, and another brings him into contact with Man Singh, it is evident that tradition ascribed him to the sixteenth century, which is probably quite near enough to the truth.[19]

The next instance belongs to the twentieth century. A few years ago there died in the village of Eral, in Tinnevelly District, a local gentleman of the Shanar caste named Arunachala Naḍar. There was nothing remarkable about his career: he had lived a highly respectable life, scrupulously fulfilled his religious duties, and served with credit as chairman of the municipal board in his native village. If he had done something prodigiously wicked, one might have expected him to become a local god at once, in accordance with Dravidian precedent; but he being what he was, his post-mortem career is rather curious. For a legend gradually arose that his kindly spirit haunted a certain place, and little by little it has grown until now there is a regular worship of him in Eral, and pilgrims travel thither to receive his blessings, stimulated by a lively literary propaganda. He is worshipped under the name of "The Chairman God," in affectionate memory of his municipal career, and as Jagadisa, or "Lord of the Universe," a phase of the god Siva.

Endnotes

1. See H. Raychaudhuri, *Materials for the Study of the Early History of the Vaishnava Sect, p. 27.*

2. It must be admitted that ancient writers give different etymologies of the name: thus, a poet in the Mahabharata (III. clxxxix. 3) derives it from *nara* , "waters," and *ayanam*, "going," understanding it to mean "one who has the waters for his resting-place"; Manu (I. 10, with Medhatithi's commentary), accepting the same etymology, interprets it as "the dwelling-place of all the Naras"; and in the Mahabharata XII. cccxli. 39, it is also explained as "the dwelling-place of mankind." But these interpretations are plainly artificial concoctions.

3. RV. X. cxxix. 5, SB. VI. i. 1, 1-5. Cf. Charpentier, *Suparnasage*, p. 387.

4. It is obvious that this island lies in a latitude somewhere between that of Lilliput and Brobdingnag, and that the professors who have endeavoured to locate it on the map of Asia have wasted their time.

5. See Rapson, *Ancient India*, p. 156 ff., *Cambridge Hist. India*, i, pp. 521, 558, 625, H. Ray Chaudhuri, *Materials for the Study of the Early History of the Vaishnava Sect*, p. 59, and Ramaprasad Chanda, *Archæology and Vaishnava Tradition* in *Memoirs of the Archæological Survey of India*, No. 5, p. 151 ff., etc.

6. See R. Chanda, *ut supra*, p. 152 f.

7. It is noteworthy that Samkarshana is here mentioned first, as is also the case in the Nanaghat inscription of about 100 B.C., which mentions them as descendants of the Moon in a list of various deities. This order may possibly be due to the fact that in ancient legend Saṃkarshana, or Bala-bhadra, is the elder brother of Kṛishna Vasudeva, and it does not entitle us to draw the inference that he ever received equal honour with Vasudeva. Special devotees of Saṃkarshana are mentioned in the Kauṭiliya, the famous treatise on polity ascribed to Chanakya, the minister of Chandra-gupta Maurya, who came to the throne about 320 B.C. (Engl. transl. 1st edn., p. 485). I suspect that in its present form the Kauṭiliya is considerably later than 320 B.C.; but in any case the existence of special votaries of Saṃkarshana is no proof that he ever ranked as equal to Vasudeva, just as the presence of special worshippers of Arjuna is no proof that Arjuna was ever considered a peer of Vasudeva. On the Ghasundi inscription see R. Chanda, *ut supra*, p. 163 ff., etc.; for the Nanaghat inscription, *ibidem* and *Memoirs of the Arch. Survey of India*, No. 1, with H. Raychaudhuri's *Materials, etc.*, p. 68 ff.

8. R. Chanda, *ut supra*, p. 169 f.

9. R. Chandra, *ut supra*, p. 165 f.

10. Rapson, *Catal. of the Coins of the Andhra Dynasty, etc.*, pp. xliv, lxii, lxix, cxxxiii-cxxxvi, clxii; *Indian Antiq.*, xlvii, p. 85, etc.

11. I regret that I cannot accept the ingenious hypothesis lately put forward by Rai Saheb Dineshchandra Sen in his *Bengali Ramayanas*. The story of the Dasaratha-jataka seems to me to be a garbled and bowdlerised snippet cut off from a possibly pre-Valmikian version of the old Rama-saga; the rest of the theory appears to be quite mistaken.

12. On this name see above, p. 86.

13. The student may refer to Sir R. G. Bhandarkar's *Vai navas and Saivas* (in Bühler's *Grundriss*, p. 74 ff.,) J. N. Farquhar's *Outline of the Relig. Liter. of India*, p. 234 f., 298 ff., and my *Heart of India*, p. 60 ff., for some details on these poets.

14. See Farquhar, *ut supra*, p. 323 ff.; *Heart of India*, p. 49 f., etc.

15. Those are at Pushkar in Rajputana, Dudahi in Bundelkhand, Khed Brahma in Idar State, and Kodakkal in Malabar.

16. This idea in germ is already suggested in Maitr. Upan., IV. 5 f., and V. 2.

17. See Vasudevananda Sarasvati's *Datta-purana* and Ganesa Narayana Karve's *Dattatreya-sarvasva*.

18. On these figures see Gopinatha Rau, *Elements of Hindu Iconography*, i. p. 252 ff. The dogs seem to be connected with the Vēdic Saramā, on whom see Charpentier, *Die Suparṇasage*, p. 91.

19. See Dineshchandra Sen, *Folk-literature of Bengal*, p. 99 ff.

CONCLUSION

Can we trace any uniform principle running through the bewildering variety of changes that we have observed?

Consider the changes through which Vishnu has passed. At the beginning a spirit of vaguely defined personality, he appears successively as a saviour-god, as the mystic saint Narayana, as the epic warriors Krishna and Rama, as a wanton blue-skinned herd-boy fluting and dancing amidst a crowd of wildly amorous women, and as the noble ideal of God preached by the great Maratha and Ramanandi votaries, not to mention the many other incarnations that have delighted the Hindu imagination. What does all this mean? It means that the history of a god is mainly moulded by two great factors, the growth of the people's spiritual experience and the character of its religious teachers. As the stream of history rolls on, it fills men's souls with deeper and wider understanding of life. Old conceptions are pondered upon, explored, tested, sometimes rejected, sometimes accepted with a new and profounder content, and thus enlarged they are applied to the old ideals of godhead. When Indian society had organised itself out of tribal chaos and settled down under an established monarchical government, it made Indra the king of the gods, ruling with the same forms and under the same conditions as a human sovereign. When men of finer cast realised that the kingdom of the spirit is higher than earthly royalty, they turned away from Indra and set their souls upon greater conceptions, ideals of vaster spiritual forces, mystic infinitudes. Attracted thus to worships such as those of Siva and Vishnu, they filled them with their own visions and imparted to these gods the ideals of their own strivings, making them into Yogisvaras, Supreme Mystics. And so the sequence of change has gone on through the generations. Most potently it has been effected by the characters of the preachers and teachers of religion. Almost every teacher who has a personality of his own, whose soul contains thoughts other than those of the common sort, stamps something of his own type upon the ideal of his god which he imparts to his followers, and which may thereby come to be authoritatively recognised as a canonical character of the god. India is peculiarly liable to this transference of personality from the guru to the god whom the guru preaches, because from immemorial times India has regarded the guru as representative of the god, and often deifies him as a permanent phase of the deity. Saivas declare that in the guru who teaches the way of salvation Siva himself is manifested: Vaishnavas tell the same tale, and find a short road to salvation by surrendering their souls to him. We have seen cases of apotheosis of the guru in modern and medieval times; reasoning from the known to the unknown, we may be sure that it took place no less regularly in ancient ages, and brought about most of the surprising changes in the character of gods which we have noticed. Sometimes the gurus have only preached some new features in the characters of their gods; sometimes, as is the Hindu fashion, they have also exhibited in their own persons, their dress and equipment, their original ideas of divinity, as, for example, Lakulisa with his club; and their sanctity and apotheosis have ratified their innovations in theology and iconology, which have spread abroad as their congregations have grown. Thus the gurus and their congregations have made the history of their deities, recasting the gods ever anew in the mould of man's hopes and strivings and ideals. There is much truth in the saying of the Brahmanas: "In the beginning the gods were mortal."

www.ingramcontent.com/pod-product-compliance
Lightning Source LLC
Chambersburg PA
CBHW072011170626
46813CB00005B/2115